LITTLE LOST DOLLS

H.C. MARIE

Book Cover by Anna Rose at The Bloodied Soul Creative

Edited by Emilie Mortali at Glitter Penned Edits

Illustrations by Greenie at that.green.critter

Character art by Kari Artik

CONTENTS

TRIGGER WARNING

Breeding kink

Cannibalism

Explicit sexual scenes and language

Human trafficking

Mentions of miscarriage

Murder

Sexual assault

Somnophillia

Stockholm Syndrome

Violence

DEDICATION

To the women who refuse to be broken or bend under a man's control. Sometimes the best revenge is finding a man (or two) who will love and protect you fiercely. Let the feminine rage demand its own vengeance.

PROLOGUE

BECKETT

I run my fingers through my curly hair as I watch Esmarie through my computer screens, just as I do every day. She doesn't know I'm watching her, but it's my job to watch over her. I made a promise that I'd use my skills to keep her safe. Watching her through monitors is the best way I can ensure that without blowing the cover of her carefully curated life. Her father isn't aware of just how far I've gone to keep my promise to him.

A normal person would feel guilty or perhaps a bit disturbed if they were constantly watching someone's life play out on a screen. I'm no stalker; don't get it twisted. I'm perhaps overzealous in my efforts to watch over her.

Our fathers are childhood best friends. It's crazy that we live two completely different lives. I'm a tech nerd and hacker for BeauCrest, a secret society founded by the Beaumont's. It houses the best mercenaries, hackers, and weapons development in the world. BeauCrest Solutions is the legal front of our operations; one of the largest tech empires. Esmarie is clueless about our world and off living her life as an accessory to Tatum fucking Carter.

Esmarie could do so much more with her life. She graduated top of her class from an Ivy League college. She had the next ten years planned out by the time she was accepted into grad school. Then, William introduced her to Tatum. The next thing I know, she dropped out to play the role of a doting live-in girlfriend. Within the year, Tatum proposed. Unfortunately for me, she said yes.

Truthfully, Esmarie should be preparing to run the Beaumont empire. She should be right here with me, knowing I exist. It's nothing more than a mere dream that I'd be so ingrained in her life as I am in hers; that she'd crave me as much as I crave her. Emmett Beaumont has many enemies, and someone close to him is undermining us all.

After his wife, Harper, was murdered, Emmett took drastic precautionary measures. He changed his daughter's last name and sent her to live with his half-brother. Emmett asked his best friend, my father, to watch over Esmarie if his enemies won, or if anything was to happen to him.

My father manages her finances and oversees the secret trust her mother left behind for her. I'm in charge of her security and surveillance. Since my skills are primarily technological and not in firearms or combat, I track her through cameras while a trusted member lurks in the shadows, acting as a hidden bodyguard. If she's aware of his presence, she has given no indication that she's noticed.

I trace the outline of her face as I watch her try on wedding dresses through the bridal boutique's surveillance cameras. Her dark auburn hair hangs in soft ringlets. I can envision her so perfectly. I want so badly to be close enough to count every one of her freckles. Filled with so much longing, I think I'm going insane. It should be me she's picking the perfect dress for.

She seems happy enough with Tatum. He's never hit her, and he provides for her. Maybe Esmarie's shallow and materialistic enough to be content with that. The version of Esmarie in my head would need so much more than settling for a guy like Tatum. I fear the day our worlds collide and we finally meet. What if she doesn't live up to the expectations I've built for her in my dreams? But what if she's so much more?

CHAPTER 1

Esmarie

"Suck it in, Esmarie. It's not zipping! Brielle, come give me a hand!" my sister hisses.

Fuck. Fuck. FUCK! This can't be happening. Anastasia tugs roughly on my dress as my best friend desperately tries to zip up the ivory lace. I suck in as much as physically possible. I can handle my dress pinching for the night.

A round of cheers marks their success in zipping me into my wedding gown. Delicate lace laid over the form fitting mermaid silhouette. A rouched bodice accentuates my waist. The off the shoulder straps pinch slightly, restricting my arm movement. That's fine; I shouldn't have to lift my arms that much on my wedding day, right?

I breathe out a sigh of relief. Everything is just fine—

The screech of my dress ripping echoes through the otherwise silent room. Opening my eyes, I survey the damage. The seam along my right hip has burst along with the bottom portion of the bodice.

How the hell could this have happened? I had my final fitting two days ago, and everything was perfect! I refuse to cry. Ruining the makeup that took hours would just be another thing on the list of shit that went wrong on what is supposed to be the happiest day of my life. The hair and makeup artists gushed over everyone else in my bridal party while giving me the cold shoulder. They acted as if I were a burden, poking at my insecurities while making them work significantly harder to make me look halfway decent. Brielle gives a pitying look before quietly excusing herself. I want nothing less than to be left alone with these people.

"Has anyone heard from Dad yet? Please tell me he's here somewhere," I question my sister and coordinator.

"Nope. Sorry, sis, but he's still MIA," Anastasia replies, far too chipper considering the circumstances.

Sensing my impending mental breakdown, Brielle excuses herself to grab her sewing kit. My sister shoos my bridesmaids out, leaving me alone in the room to have a moment to collect myself instead of cracking under the mask I've been fighting to keep on. This is a disaster. Maybe this is a sign I shouldn't go through with this wedding. Don't get me wrong, Tatum is a nice guy. He's loyal and he's financially secure. I suppose to most, that should make me happy enough, but I'm just not entirely sure he's "the one".

I'm sure Anastasia would jump at the chance to take my spot. Sometimes this marriage feels like a business arrangement my father set up, but then Tatum promises he loves me. Even though Tatum and I dated before my father pressed for marriage, Ana isn't subtle with her comments that since she's older, it should be her instead.

I'm not sure if Ana wants a marriage with Tatum specifically, or to be the first one married off. I know he would never cheat on me, but I wouldn't put it past my sister to try to seduce him. Admittedly, I'm not sure I would really care if he fell into her trap. Sure, my ego would be a little bruised, but there's a voice in the back of my head reveling in the fact that it would be an easy way out. Saying I caught my fiancé in bed with my sister would be a valid excuse to call off the wedding rather than trying to explain the chaos in my head giving me cold feet.

It's not that I don't love Tatum; I just love the man he was when we first met more than the man he's grown into. Our relationship was a whirlwind romance until it wasn't. Instead of being exhilarating like it once was, it's simply lackluster.

In the beginning, Tatum was attentive, delivering a strong sense of companionship. The moment his ring slipped onto my finger like the shackle it's become, his efforts died. He no longer had to impress me. His expectations swiftly piled up. Tatum Carter doesn't want a partner. He wants a prize on his arm, boosting his ego and status. Behind closed doors, he's indifferent at best, treating me as if I'm nothing more than a servant catering to him.

Sometimes it feels like I'm begging for scraps of his affection. He always has some excuse or just accuses me of being needy when I ask for more. Just when I feel like I've had enough, he surprises me with gifts and romantic getaways. It's a never-ending cycle of chasing the highs that the good times bring.

I wanted to become a lawyer, but that dream was put on hold. Tatum thinks the woman's place is at home, and no wife of his will be working. He is more than capable of providing for me, and I want for nothing. It's easier for him to buy my love than to just love me.

Anytime I bring these concerns up with friends and family, they tell me I'm being too harsh. I need to give it time. On paper, he's the perfect guy. They tell me I'm lucky to have a man like that interested in me. Their assurances are backhanded, as if I'm the one who's lacking.

Tatum is conventionally handsome with a thin yet muscular build. I wish he would grow out his blonde hair. You can't run your fingers through a buzz cut. He's the nice guy in everyone's eyes, and I'm ridiculed anytime I want the bare minimum. I feel trapped in this bubble of what everyone thinks my life should be. More and more each day, I have the sinking feeling I'm settling.

Three quick knocks on the door bring me out of my spiraling thoughts. My wedding coordinator peeks her head in. Right behind her, Brielle slips into the room with a black garment bag.

"Ms. Kensington, we are out of time. You have five minutes to be down there. Is there someone else who can walk you down the aisle?" she kindly asks.

Resigned, I decline. "I'll walk alone."

She offers a sad smile before softly clicking the door shut behind her. Brielle has a mischievous smile as she takes a pair of shears and cuts me out of the lace cocoon. Within minutes, a new, sleek backless satin gown fits my body like a glove.

Brielle designed a dress for me to change into for the reception. It was supposed to be a surprise, but now it's my saving grace. Tatum was the one who insisted I wear a name brand gown and not something designed by my best friend.

Brielle outdid herself. The plunging neckline offers the perfect hint of sexiness to the elegant design. I run my fingertips along the delicate crystals sewn into the drop waist corset. As I step closer to the mirror, I can see the high slit in the satin ivory fabric.

With one last glance in the mirror, I know this gown is perfect. I should have put my foot down and not even considered any other dress. Together, Brielle and I make our way down to the entrance. The wedding coordinator intercepts me with my bouquet, which is thankfully intact. Brielle winks before she waltzes off to complete the wedding processional as I stand off to the side, hidden from view.

Tatum stands stoically at the pew, looking bored. I always imagined my future husband holding back tears of joy when he saw me walking down the aisle. Instead, my soon to be husband is checking the time on the gold Patek Philippe watch my father gifted him at our engagement party, as if he has somewhere better to be. There's a flash of surprise and anger on Ana's face when she notices the dress I'm wearing. Like the pro she is, she masks it quickly. Maybe she expected me to march out in a torn dress. Better yet, she likely wanted me to be discouraged enough to call off the whole wedding entirely.

Alone, I strut my way down to the instrumental of "Video Games" by Lana Del Rey. It's not the boring traditional song Tatum wanted. This was a last minute change, no doubt of my best friend's doing to make the recessional more bearable. Brielle offers an encouraging smile, whereas Ana looks borderline hysterical with how gleeful she's trying to appear. She's probably loving this train wreck. She's the leader of an entirely one-sided sister rivalry. I truly want the best for her; I just want her off my back.

CHAPTER 2

ESMARIE

The rock on my finger mocks me. It's a stunning four carat oval cut diamond. It feels like lead weighing me down as it glistens under the extravagant chandelier. This wedding reception is nothing I would have planned for myself. Looking around the expansive room, I recognize very few faces. Most of the attendees are business partners and friends of Tatum and my father.

Mechanically, I make the rounds greeting guests on my husband's arm. Plastering a fake smile on my face, no one knows me well enough to see through the facade. Empty congratulations follow me, and I gracefully accept each one, all while hoping I didn't just make a terrible mistake. When asked about the honeymoon destination, Tatum brushes it off with ease. He pats my hand while saying, "It's a surprise for the wife." I look at him, hoping he will let a clue slip, just to ease a fraction of my anxiety.

I packed my necessities myself, but Tatum assured me his assistant packed the rest accordingly. I'm not sure why he is so adamant that I don't know where we are honeymooning. He knows I hate surprises. I even asked Brielle, hoping she at least knew, but she's just as clueless.

I continue going through the motions as people bustle around me. I space out completely during the best man's speech and only snap out of it when a chorus of laughter erupts during Brielle's speech.

My sister, to no one's surprise, opted out of giving a speech. Tatum bristles beside me when Brielle recounts stories from our college days. Just like everything she does, her love shines through her words.

Tatum effortlessly leads me through our first dance to "You and Me" by Lifehouse. Once the song finishes, I look around for my father. I'd be delusional to think he'd show up in time for the father and daughter dance. Embarrassment heats my cheeks, and I awkwardly make my way back to my seat with what I hope is a reassuring smile. Tatum wastes no time flaunting his mother around for their dance

As I sit at the table watching my husband, envious that his parents are here for him, Anastasia leans in conspiratorially. "How unfortunate Father couldn't be here for your special day. His wedding was so much more extravagant than this. He's having the time of his life on his honeymoon, while poor Esmarie's forgotten."

I look at her in shock. "What do you mean married and on his honeymoon? How do you know?"

"I was at the wedding, obviously. Plus, he texted me earlier. He must've forgotten to let you know." She shrugs as if it's no big deal.

I brace my hands on the seat to make sure it's just the room spinning around me. My father got married and never mentioned it. Worse yet, I didn't get invited. Yet, Anastasia seems to have been. Plus, he had the time to text her and update her on his whereabouts yet couldn't bother to send a courtesy text letting me know he wouldn't be here to walk me down the aisle like he promised. Father and Anastasia have always been closer, I just wish he would love me the same. Perhaps he blames me for the car crash that killed his wife. The scar on my hip may be faded, but they never let me forget how I got it.

The song finishes and Tatum returns. Seeing my expression, he gives Ana an accusatory glare before pushing a glass of water my way.

"Look, Esmarie, I have a business meeting after this, so I won't be flying out with you. I'll meet you there in a few days though, I promise," he admits softly.

What does he mean he has a business meeting? He schedules his own meetings. Our wedding and honeymoon have been planned for months! He had ample time to plan accordingly. This entire reception is one big business meeting with all his partners, for fuck's sake! What the actual fuck is happening today? I don't think I can handle anything else going wrong.

I feel the familiar signs of an anxiety attack. My hands are clammy, my chest is tight, and I'm precariously close to crying. I excuse myself from the table. Once I'm out of sight of the guests, I take off running in search of a private alcove. I lose track of time as I regain my composure, all while wondering how things could have gone so terribly wrong.

As I'm making my way back to the reception area, I hear Tatum's familiar deep baritone. The words are barely discernible, but my sister's unmistakably nasally voice leaches from behind closed doors. I'm not sure why my sister and husband would be hiding away in a back room having a conversation, but I can't find it in me to care.

He's never given any indication of being unfaithful, let alone that there's anything going on between the two of them. What's sad is I don't think I'd care either way. My sister loves the challenge of gaining the attention of married men. She's beautiful with her long, silky straight blonde hair and long model-like legs.

Tatum's frustrated voice is clear as day when he says, "It doesn't matter, Ana. We won't have to worry about her much longer. She won't be returning from the honeymoon, and it'll be my right as her husband to sort out her finances and the trust she just inherited."

The gasp escapes me before I remember I'm eavesdropping. What the hell are they talking about? I don't have an inheritance. For the first time, I'm scared of Tatum. Nothing good can come from the promise I won't return from our honeymoon. I have to get out of here. As I turn to run, I catch sight of Tatum with a wicked smile plastered on his face before running into a solid wall of muscle.

"Tsk tsk Esmarie. You never could mind your own business," my sister scolds as I feel a prick on my neck.

My hand rushes up on instinct. The world around me blurs.

"Well, I suppose this just makes things easier," I vaguely hear Tatum mumble.

The world around me goes black. Someone catches me just as I collapse.

CHAPTER 3

BECKETT

Alarm bells are ringing. Something is very wrong. Typically, I don't like to dig into the lives of Esmarie's acquaintances to not invade their privacy. I should have known better and put my morals aside. Maybe if I did, then I could've protected my girl better.

I set up a program to flag anyone who searches for Esmarie, anything related to Mr. Beaumont, and the trust fund she has gained access to. Someone has been sniffing around Esmarie. Last I knew, Esmarie herself wasn't even aware of the trust fund waiting for her. Only Mr. Beaumont's trusted inner circle has the exclusive knowledge of Esmarie's relocation, hidden identity, and the legacy Mr. Beaumont secured for her.

Two names have consistently been flagged in my system. Anastasia Kensington and Tatum goddamn Carter. Anastasia's jealousy of her sister is more than apparent in her text exchanges with Tatum. Thankfully for him, he's ignored all her advances so far. Esmarie deserves nothing but complete and utter devotion and loyalty. After a bit more digging, I found flight confirmations in Tatum's email. There's a one-way ticket to Montenegro for Esmarie tonight. My stomach sinks. Tatum didn't book a ticket for himself to Montenegro at all. No, he booked round trip tickets for him and Anastasia two days later to Mykonos. They, of course, are booked on a private jet, whereas Esmarie gets economy.

Why on earth would he not accompany his wife on their honeymoon? Better yet, why do he and Anastasia have coordinating tickets? Worse, why only a one-way ticket for her? Anxiety coils in my stomach as I debate on digging further into what he has planned or to go and try to intercept her before she boards that plane.

I try calling Bruce, who is the head of her security detail. He should always have eyes on her. He's her shadow, after all. After the third call goes to voicemail, I panic. It's unlike him to dodge my calls. I call my father to prepare the private jet. Haphazardly, I toss some clothes, a suit, and my laptop into a bag

My father pulls up to my security gate, and I'm rushing through before the car has enough clearance to drive through. I pull my suit out of the bag and tug it on in the backseat as my father drives us to Mr. Beaumont's private airstrip. Five of our executive security team are already waiting for us as we pull up. I toss my hand up in a rushed greeting before climbing the stairs. I toss myself into the first seat and immediately fire up my laptop.

According to the itinerary, the wedding ceremony is over, and they are an hour into the reception. It's only a two hour flight from New York City to Montreal. I should have plenty of time to crash the reception, find Bruce, and stop Esmarie from getting on that plane.

Within minutes, I've hacked into the reception venue's security feed. My screen's split into twelve different video feeds. I scan through each one, searching for her beautiful dark auburn hair; or the only one wearing a white dress. She stands out like a beacon in the night. My girl has her dress bundled in her hands as she wanders around, trying to open doors until she finally comes across one that was unlocked. She looks frantic in her pursuit.

I'm not sure what could have caused her to run away like that. I search through the cameras for Tatum. Surely if his bride ran off, he would be hot on her heels to comfort her. He is still in the reception hall, completely unaware his bride is hiding. Brielle is the first to notice her absence.

Given the tense body language, I'm sure Brielle is confronting Tatum for being too busy to notice his wife is nowhere to be found. Brielle stomps off, and I'm thankful she has someone in her corner. In no time, she finds the room Esmarie is hiding in. A few minutes go by before Brielle leaves, likely placated by the excuse of 'just needing to get away from the chaos for a bit'. Esmarie stays in that room for over an hour, uninterrupted.

Just as the pilot announces that we're preparing for landing, Tatum and Anastasia pass by one of the security cameras with their heads bowed close together. With her stilettos, Anastasia is not much shorter than Tatum's six-foot stature. They find a room to slip into much easier than Esmarie's desperate search.

I stumble down the stairs of the jet with my laptop still in hand. My father helps guide me to the awaiting armored Cadillac. His face is etched with worry. While everyone recruited for this rescue mission knows what's at stake, my father is the only one implicitly as protective of Esmarie as I am.

The GPS says we are still forty-five minutes away from the venue. Esmarie carefully exits her hiding spot. I anxiously bite my fingernails as I watch Esmarie make her way to the room Tatum and Anastasia are hiding in. Where the hell are Bruce and his team? I turn to Liam, who I've been training. He thankfully has his laptop out and is just getting into the venue's video feed.

"Any eyes on Bruce?" I question with a hint of desperation.

"Got him! He's hiding out in the kitchen," Liam exclaims.

"Why the hell is he in the kitchen? He should always have eyes on his mark!" I huff out.

My father nods his agreement; the furrow in his brow may as well be a permanent fixture. Something Esmarie overhears startles her, and she stumbles away from the door.

"Bruce got a text," Liam starts before comparing our screens. "Oh good. He's heading Esmarie's way."

I look around the team huddled in the Cadillac. Maybe someone texted him to get back to his mark, and I missed it. They all shake their heads at my questioning gaze. My stomach drops as Tatum and Anastasia exit the room. Whatever Esmarie overheard caused Tatum to drop his nice guy facade. The malice on their faces is unmistakable, even through the cameras.

An audible sigh leaves my lips as I see Bruce approaching Esmarie from behind, and I slouch back into my seat. Bruce is going to get my girl away from them. That's wishful thinking though, because arms whip out anchoring me in my seat. All I can do is stare in horror as I watch Bruce pull a syringe from his pocket and inject its contents into Esmarie's neck.

Bruce gives Tatum a curt nod as Esmarie sways on her feet. For a moment, I'm unsure if anyone will make a move to break her fall or help guide her to the ground. Bruce, at least, catches her. But then, he tosses her limp body carelessly over his shoulder.

Even if we broke almost every traffic law in Montreal, we would still be fifteen minutes too late. Tracing Bruce's path, he's carrying Esmarie to a waiting car stationed at the back entrance. Dread feasts on my insides. We are going to be too late. Once they get in the car, they could take a number of paths to the airport. I don't have time for the mental breakdown fighting to consume me over the fact that we are going to be too late to save her.

Defeated, I log into an account I never thought I'd have to access. When Esmarie was born, Emmett had a tracking device hidden in a cap added to the femoral head of her hip. It would take the equivalent of a hip replacement surgery to remove it. When Esmarie was old enough to ask questions about the scar, William told her she was with his late wife in a car accident and was impaled by a piece of shrapnel during the collision. . While his wife didn't make it, that scar was proof that she survived.

Tatum must've called for his own private jet, because they are going the opposite direction of the Montreal International Airport. We abandon the route to the venue in an attempt to catch them before they can enter the likely private airfield. How else are they going to board an unconscious woman?

"Son, if we can't stop them before they depart, we'll have no choice but to wait until they land. We don't know if they are still taking her to Montenegro, or if they even were to begin with. Plus, we can't exactly follow her in the air," my father laments with a hand braced on my shoulder.

It's not what I want to hear, but I know he's right. We sit in silence with one question lingering between us. How the hell did they flip Bruce?

CHAPTER 4

ESMARIE

My eyelids feel heavy as they flutter open. It takes a few minutes for my surroundings to blink into focus. A dull pressure throbs at the back of my skull. My tongue is swollen, and my mouth is so dehydrated that razor blades slice my throat with each attempted swallow.

The surrounding lights are dim, and a soft hum of an engine plays in the background. My heart rate spikes as I recount what I overheard before everything went black. Remembering the prick at the base of my neck after I ran into a boulder of a man, I instinctively reach my hand toward my neck, anticipating the bite of pain. Only my hand doesn't move.

I close my eyes and try to calm myself. My brain won't function properly if I'm having a panic attack. Focusing on my other senses, I can tell there is a seat belt strapped across my lap. Seems like I made it onto a plane after all. Zip ties restrain my wrists and ankles to the leather seat I'm buckled into.

Fear churns in my stomach until I have no other option than to turn my head as my stomach rejects its contents all over the pristine leather seat beside me.

Gagging has my eyes snapping open and searching out the source of the intruding noise. A burly bald man in all black lounges on a couch along the opposite wall.

"Fuck, that shit is vile. You couldn't just hold it in? Vomit doesn't hold the same appeal as titties, no need to free it," he grumbles, choking back another gag.

"Who the hell are you, and why am I tied to a seat?" I demand.

"I've been watching you for years, Esmarie. It's unfortunate that everyone but you noticed. As for why you're here, well, you have something they want. They just can't do that with you in the picture," he explains.

"Since it doesn't look like I'm going on my honeymoon, wanna fill me in on where I was supposed to be going?" I hedge.

"Oh, technically you're still going. You had a ticket booked to Montenegro, and someone was supposed to take you from the capital's airport straight onto a cargo train to Albania. You simply fast tracked those plans when you decided to stick your nose where it didn't belong. I can't take an unconscious girl through the airport, though. Tatum's pissed he had to waste his private jet on you," he snips.

I wasn't aware Tatum even had a private jet, let alone knew anyone that had access to one. Why? Why is this happening to me? I live a boring life. I take care of the house while I wait for Tatum to come home and hang out with Brielle on the weekends. Baldie's mocking laughter rings through the cabin of the plane. I must've asked out loud.

"You have no clue, do you? You're worth more than you or those fuckwits realize. As for why I'm delivering you like cargo, it was part of our deal. I help them out by taking you off their hands, and I have free rein to do with you as I please. If I want to sell you off, I can, and I get to keep everything I'll make from handing you over."

I'd have some serious wrinkles from frowning if it weren't for the Botox Tatum insisted I get. So, there is no honeymoon. Worse, this intimidating stranger is in charge of what happens to me next. From the sound of it, he's planning on selling me off. What could Tatum possibly gain from marrying me only for me to disappear? Anastasia's motives are easily discernible. She can be Daddy's only focus and maybe, just maybe, take my place at Tatum's side.

My stomach drops as we descend to land. Baldie pulls a syringe from his pocket.

"Are you going to behave, or do you need another dose?" he questions with an arched brow.

"I'll behave," I reluctantly agree with a shudder, remembering the needle and waking from its effects.

The last thing I need is to be at his mercy in a foreign country while unconscious. Who knows how long I was out the first time. With a glare, Baldie frees my wrists and ankles. His grip is bruising as he latches onto my upper arm to guide me off the plane to a waiting car.

Without my heels providing me the extra inches in height, the excess fabric of my dress winds around my ankles. Still disoriented, I only make it a few shuffled steps before tripping. The vise-like grip around my arm is the only thing keeping me from face planting. A hard shove to the middle of my back has me crashing into the backseat. Baldie and I sit in silence as I attempt to murder him a hundred different ways with my glare alone. I mindlessly watch the array of colors catapulting across the horizon as the sun sets into the night. It's a relatively short drive, and before I know it, we're screeching to a halt.

My last thread of hope dies. It was perhaps the delusions that made me believe we'd be going to a train station with boarding passes in hand. If I had been listening to him earlier, I would've caught his meaning when he said he was delivering me like cargo. My predicament makes sense. Unfortunately. We stop on an empty gravel road with a stopped train less than fifty feet away. One door is slightly ajar. I can't see anything past the darkness blanketing its contents.

Baldie drags me out of the car, stumbling behind him as we approach. There's no sign of anyone I can ask for help. My aching feet leave the ground. They're happy with the reprieve until I collide with metal. I skitter across the dirty cargo container. The brute fucking launched me in here like a sack of potatoes. I'm simultaneously relieved and annoyed when Baldie hoists himself in. I suppose he needs to supervise his merchandise until he has the money in hand.

Still dressed in my wedding gown, I fight against the corset pinching my ribs to curl into a ball. I angrily blink back tears, refusing to let them fall, but I'm not strong enough to fight them. I cry myself to sleep, refusing to open my eyes when the train jostles me awake. Ignoring the soft whimpers nearby, I pray that this is all just a bad dream.

CHAPTER 5

JASPER

I hate my brother for a plethora of reasons. Getting me dragged into this bullshit is right at the top of the list. How he got wrapped up in human trafficking, I'll never know. They tell me I only have one more year of servitude to repay his debts. I suspect that after the year, I'll either be dead, or deeper into this life. No one escapes unscathed.

My humanity is hanging on by a thread. Unlike most of the men under Sylvester's control, I can recognize the girls as human beings and not the objects they're being sold as. I hate referring to them as merchandise. While every man surrounding me foams at the mouth at having unlimited access to rape the girls we have locked away, my cock doesn't even twitch at the idea of getting wet.

Don't get me wrong, it's not like my cock doesn't work. It just needs to be intrigued to function properly. I wouldn't call myself asexual, but it takes a certain something to get me going; I just don't know what that something is. I haven't found the right person, and it's not from a lack of trying.

Sylvester tried piping me full of drugs to get my cock hard so I could get the job done. I'm not sure if it was a bad lot, but when my cock remained flaccid, it was enough to convince him it was broken. I wasn't about to correct him.

Sylvester, not being one to give up so easily, went as far as making me wear a strap on. I tried to go easy on the girl, but it was hard to focus with a bullet wound in my thigh. There was little I could do to make it less traumatizing for her. The least I could do was try to make it as enjoyable as possible. I lathered the silicone with lube and went as slow as possible so I wouldn't hurt her. Still, I was so horrified and disgusted I ended up puking all over the poor girl. That was the last time they tried forcing me on the girls.

Sylvester realized that not even having a gun to my head could get me to break in the new girls, so he settled on making me their jailer. While I'm still the enemy in their eyes by being their jailer; I feel like I can at least look out for them in some fragmented capacity.

***

Today is shipment day. Usually, there are five of us unloading the merchandise. Since today is a smaller load, there's only three of us. We pull on our typical balaclavas with a skull mask covering our nose and mouth. We are unidentifiable when we go retrieve shipments.

The rumbling of the train is fast approaching. The brakes screech in an attempt to slow its momentum. As soon as the train stops, we hastily search for our target. We tag all our cargo containers with a pink upside-down smiley face with a crown. Once located, we crack the door open.

Putrid fumes accumulated during their travel are immediately invading our senses. Who knows how long the girls have been trapped in their own filth. There are two men inside chatting casually, as if girls in cages are completely normal. I suppose for them, it probably is.

It's not uncommon for sellers to accompany their merchandise to us when they are trading or paying off debts. The two men are already yapping with my colleagues while they unlock the cages.

I'm carrying an unconscious girl to the van when a vision of a woman stands at the edge of the container. Her vibrant auburn hair is a stark contrast to the wedding dress she still has on. I wonder if her new husband was the one who delivered her to this fate.

I'm captivated by her. My eyes track her as I tuck the girl away and lock up the van so they can't escape when I go to retrieve the next girl. I'm entranced as I take in every miniscule movement she makes. I wonder if she is bold enough to attempt making a run for it. Fuck, I wish she would, just so I have an excuse to chase her.

With her chin up, she clambers her way down from the train. A bald man that must've been traveling with her must say something because her head snaps his way. Her lip twitches in a snarl before she stomps my way. Once her back is to him, the ferocity melts away as panic overtakes her features.

She makes it three steps before her legs get tangled in her dress and she's falling face first to the muddy ground. My feet reflexively move. Before either of us is aware, she's cradled in my arms. The poor thing is trembling in my grip. Faint traces of something sweet and spicy lingers in her hair. My cock twitches in my cargo pants, and if I didn't have to put on a facade, my eyes would roll to the back of my head at the hit of arousal.

"I need a favor. Can you get a hold of whoever is in charge here?" she implores hesitantly.

I'm speechless that she's talking to me, let alone asking a favor. It only piques my curiosity more. Her hazel eyes bore into mine, and I have half a mind to nod in response. She clutches the collar of my jacket, pulling me closer into her orbit.

"The bald man who came with me, I don't want him profiting by bringing me here. I know there's no chance of me going home. That's fine. Keep me, just don't give him whatever he's supposed to get for me," she pleads in a whisper

My girl is a spiteful little spitfire. I love it. I hope her spirit isn't broken too much over the next few weeks. By the end of the month, she'll be sold at the next auction.

"I'm going to put you in the van, and I'll make a call," I offer.

With a nod, she wiggles out of my hold and strides over to the van. She hops into the passenger seat and holds out a hand expectantly. With an arched brow, I toss her a pair of handcuffs. She latches the first cuff around her wrist, looking at me expectantly. Once I pull my phone out, she hooks the other cuff around the grab handle.

Turning my back to her, I subtly adjust my rigid cock into my waistband to hide her effect on me. I make my way back to the train and ask the bald man his name for verification. The other guys give me a questioning look before returning to their conversation. After three rings, Sylvester answers.

"Hey Boss, sorry to bother you. I have a Bruce here handing over a girl. She has an obscure request I thought would interest you. She's accepted she's stuck with us but doesn't want Bruce to profit off her," I explain.

"A bald prick?"

"Yes, Boss."

"Is the girl going to be a problem?"

"I don't think so, Boss. She willingly cuffed herself in the car. I think she's just spiteful."

"Fine, take care of him. Saves me 10K," he concedes with a hint of annoyance.

The line disconnects before I can reply. I'd be more annoyed that he hung up on me if it weren't for the fact he gave me the green light to end this prick. I meet a pair of hazel eyes. Seems like she's watching me as much as I have her. I pull the door open and come face to face with the little spitfire.

"Listen to me carefully, little hellion. I'm going to take care of Bruce over there for you. You need to close your eyes and cover your ears for me, all right?" I all but beg.

"You mean Baldie? The asshole was working with my husband. Do you think I can file for an annulment?" she ponders, ignoring my request.

I blink at her. Is she for real? She's basically being kidnapped, and she's asking about an annulment. At least I'm not about to murder her husband. That wouldn't give me any brownie points. Or maybe it would, given she doesn't hide her animosity toward Bruce. I'm unsure why I'm suddenly so worried about what one of the trafficked girls thinks of me. For once, I care about how I'm perceived. I don't want her to be scared of me.

"Just do as you're told. Please?"

With a dramatic sigh, she pinches her eyes shut and covers her ears by palming one with her hand and leaning into the inside of her cuffed arm. I admire her for a moment before striding over to Bruce. I offer a curt nod to my guys before firing off a round into his kneecap.

He howls out in pain, cursing me, screaming that the little cunt isn't worth this. Sylvester was right; Bruce is a prick. With a wicked smile that will haunt him in hell, I fire one more shot between his eyes. As he crumples to the ground, I take the last girl from the cage and escort her to the van. Before they can question me, I wave my phone in the air, indicating it was Sylvester's orders.

After locking the last girl in the back of the van, my little hellion is trembling in her seat. A defeated sigh escapes me as I turn the ignition and leave the others to clean up the mess. I'll send a car for them.

Part of me wishes to know my little hellion's name, but I know it'll make things more difficult. I can't be humanizing her. If she thinks my murdering her abductor is bad, she has no clue what kind of hell awaits her.

CHAPTER 6

ESMARIE

My wrist aches as we drive through back roads. The gunshots echo through my mind. Maybe I was a bit too rash in offering myself as a willing sacrifice so long as Baldie didn't profit from my suffering. How was I supposed to know my request meant his death? I suppose these aren't normal people or circumstances.

I could be delusional, but I suspect the man in the mask doesn't want me to be afraid of him. I mean, he didn't move me to the back of the van with the other girls; not that I gave him much of a choice. Tingles zap down my arm where it's pulled numbly above my head. I do my best to get some sleep on the drive. Every time I'm about to doze off, the feeling of being watched wakes me. When my eyes open, I catch his eyes already on me before he can avert his gaze.

After what feels like hours, the van idles in front of an abandoned shed on the edge of the rugged wilderness. We sit in silence before he climbs out. He strides in front of the van, making his way toward the shed. Rumbling fills the surrounding air before a beat-up Jeep pulls from the confines of a shed. His confident strides carry him to me.

He unlatches the cuff, and my arm falls limply to my side. Massaging my sore wrist delivers no relief. Before I can make sense of what's happening, an arm latches around my waist, casually carrying me to our new ride. As if on autopilot, he cuffs my wrist to the interior of the Jeep's door before transferring the girls to the back. Spinning in my seat, the severity of my situation sinks in. They removed the back seats and transformed the entire back into a large cage.

He parks the van in the shed before switching vehicles. We pull back onto the road, and I watch time pass by through the clock on the radio. Two hours drag on before I can't take it anymore and focus my attention on the scenery. We turn off onto a side road, where the road rapidly thins out as we drive deeper into the tree line. Soon, there's no clear road for him to follow, just a worn path scarring the terrain from the numerous treks.

At last, the tree line breaks. Lying in the middle of a clearing is a log cabin. It looks lonely and abandoned out here. Negative energy emanates from it, churning my stomach.

Turning in my seat, I look at him nervously. He removes the outer skull mask covering the lower half of his face. The only distinguishable feature I've seen was his honey brown eyes. Part of me isn't ready to let go of the mystery. His hand lifts to remove his balaclava. I lift my hand to his face, stopping him before he can pull it up any further.

As we stare at each other, lost in the moment, I blink back tears. The trance is broken as he wraps a large hand around my wrist. The first and only tear falls as he gently strokes my wrist with his thumb. With a defeated sigh, he pulls my hand away from his face. Cradling my hand in his against his chest, his heart pounds ferociously in his chest.

In a series of swift movements, he has my free hand locked in the last cuff, and his balaclava grasped tightly in his hand by his side. His eyes are pinched closed as if our reality hurts him as much as it hurts me. He is breathtakingly handsome with his five o'clock shadow. His wavy onyx hair is shorter on the sides and longer on top. When he finally pries his eyes open, the pity in them tells me we both know what seeing his face means. They aren't concerned about my being able to identify them, because I won't be leaving here alive.

My world is tilted upside down as he tosses me over his shoulder. Lifting my head, a group of men exit the building. They quickly and efficiently unload the girls from the back of the Jeep.

The other girls were on the train much longer than I was. I was lucky considering Baldie fed me on the train. I tried to share my food with the other girls, but I only shared with two before he was up and shoving the rest down my throat. Their emaciated state is obvious in the way they have no energy to fight against the men. A few are so weak they have to be carried inside.

A whistle cuts through the air. "Jasper, mind grabbing the last one from the back?" one of the leather clad men asks.

I finally have a name. Jasper.

He freezes momentarily, clearly frustrated they gave away his name. Jasper makes quick work dragging the last girl from the back of the cage. He drags her along like she's nothing while I'm being carried over his shoulder. A sick sense of unease fills me at the noticeable difference in the way we are being regarded so far.

Jasper takes us up the stairs and through the entrance. Thankfully, he takes mercy on the girl he was dragging along and slung her over his other shoulder.

The hallways are an intricate maze, intent on disorienting newcomers. If we wanted to escape, it would be near impossible to find our way through. As we descend through a stairwell, it is clear they built this cabin to suit their sick needs. A keypad lock equips the looming metal door waiting for us.

Uncaring that I can see the keypad, he punches in the code. *9491*. I carve the number into the recesses of my memory, unwilling to forget it.

As he descends the stairs, his hand creeps further up my thigh. His hand stops precariously close to my ass before locking onto me tightly.

The girl lets out a groan as we are jostled around. My sigh of relief at the sign of life is exaggerated as my diaphragm is slammed into his shoulder on the next bounce down the stairs. Call me crazy, but I swear he murmurs an apology. Maybe there is a sliver of hope left.

Flinching when the heavy door slams behind us, Jasper continues. This floor feels more clinical than the hallway maze upstairs. While it's still an intricate series of hallways we pass through, it's significantly less intricate.

We come to a door at the end of the corridor. I can already see the biometric lock next to another large metal door. How the hell can there be another stairwell? Descending further underground, a chill permeates the air, seeping into our bones. They dug us all the way to hell.

My last inkling of hope fizzles out when what's waiting for us in the basement is exposed. The walls are lined with cells. The cells are bare except for a few buckets and tattered blankets. They're still a step up from the dog crates we were kept in on the train. Most cells have at least three girls huddled inside. At most, the cells house five girls. Very few cells are empty, and even fewer house only a single girl.

They must have a system because Jasper drops the other girl in a cell with three other equally emaciated looking girls. To my horror, I'm dropped into an empty cell.

"Welcome home, little hellion," Jasper whispers as he sets me on my feet. For once, he avoids my gaze as he locks me inside.

I wish I were back home. Obviously, I wouldn't be happy with Tatum. Our entire relationship was nothing but pretty lies that crumbled the moment I said "I do". While I would've been trapped in my marriage to Tatum, at least I'd have a comfortable little boring life inside a gilded cage. A cage is a cage, nonetheless. Now I'm wishing for it after being traded and left in this barren cell.

CHAPTER 7

BECKETT

The best part of being a member of BeauCrest is that we have headquarters dispersed across the world. Mr. Beaumont's inner circle and the higher-ranking members also know of the vast number of safe houses available to us. Since my father decided that no further action can be taken until Esmarie's flight lands, we head toward the closest safe house.

Patience is currently not a virtue I have. My foot bounces anxiously in the footwell. My eyes never leave the little red dot bouncing around. As we pull up to the inconspicuous house hidden away in a thick tree line, I don't bother packing away my things. I barely have a grip on my devices as I tear out of the car.

The first thing I do is find a room with a desk. I make quick work unloading and setting up the rest of my equipment. Liam joins me a few minutes later.

"Do you want to do a trace and see if there's been any activity regarding Esmarie or her trust?" I ask him. "Oh, and track Bruce if he hasn't ditched his phone already."

A flicker of confusion crosses his face before giving a curt nod. Cracking his knuckles, he gets to work. I leave him as he types away determinedly. I focus my attention on diving deeper into Tatum and Anastasia's correspondence and internet history. The two of them have encrypted emails with a third party. I'm fairly confident neither of them knows how to encrypt anything, so it must have been done by a third party. Even more reason for me to prioritize decrypting it.

Within minutes I'm in and scanning through the emails. The IP address matches Bruce's apartment, confirming my worst fears. I'm not a violent man, but Bruce is a dead man walking. I never imagined he would betray us like this.

My jaw clenches tighter as I piece together Tatum's motivation to marry Esmarie. Anastasia found out about the trust while snooping. Bruce simply confirmed it. She also knows that William is not Esmarie's father. That probably fed into the resentment she held toward Esmarie.

Bruce booked himself the same flight as Esmarie, and Tatum agreed to hand Esmarie off to Bruce after they landed in Montenegro. Leaving Bruce to his own devices to do as he pleases with her was a futile attempt to maintain plausible deniability of her impending disappearance.

Tatum, however, plans to weaponize their marital status to gain access to Esmarie's trust, giving Anastasia twenty percent. He's banking on using Esmarie's trust to fund the luxurious vacation he booked for the two of them. Surely, he didn't think seventy-two hours was long enough to declare her missing, dead, and have the funds of her trust transferred to him.

Anastasia, on the other hand, has offered herself up to take her sister's place as his wife. She is under the illusion that he needs a wife to maintain appearances. It's probably her backup plan if their scheme to get rich fails. Tatum denies harboring any real feelings for Esmarie. He insists it was William's influence on their relationship that made him entertain the charade with Esmarie. All this only fed her delusions further.

My heart aches for Esmarie, knowing everyone close to her never really cared for her. They so easily turned on her. Her friend, Brielle, is the only one who seems to truly care about Esmarie. For starters, the utterly stunning gown she designed for Esmarie accentuated her curves perfectly. Anyone could see the love sewn into the gown. It also took Brielle fifteen minutes to realize Esmarie wasn't in the reception hall.

Dozens of frantic messages have been sent to Esmarie, all going unanswered. They range from worry to questioning if Tatum took her away somewhere to threaten to track down William for ruining her special day.

Liam sends me a quick briefing that Tatum has already filed their marriage license and tried reporting her missing, citing her missed flight. The police, of course, told him to wait twenty-four hours to see if she turns up. Tatum's frantically trying to track down the lawyer or bank that may be managing the trust. His search history shows him looking at how long one needs to be missing before being presumed dead, and how long after death a husband can take over his deceased wife's finances. The lack of adequate planning is dumbfounding. Bruce also missed his flight. His phone is pinging in the same location as Esmarie.

Whoever he needs to contact must be important to risk us tracking his phone, or maybe he's just ignorant. Antsy, I decide now is as good a time as ever to start raising hell in the form of revenge in Esmarie's honor. With little else to look into at the moment, it's the perfect opportunity to fuck up some people's days.

I start by cancelling William's returning flight. Biological father or not, he raised Esmarie. What kind of father deliberately plans to miss his daughter's wedding after promising to be there to walk her down the aisle? Next, I file for an annulment on Esmarie's behalf. Somehow, I don't think she will be too upset about it. Finally, I schedule to have Tatum and Anastasia bank accounts and credit cards frozen the minute they scan their boarding passes for their first flight out of the country.

There's not an ounce of guilt in me for what I've done. My father lays a hand on my shoulder as he looms behind me, overlooking what I've done. He offers an encouraging smile and a nod of approval. I'm relieved, knowing he would have gone to the same lengths for Esmarie as I have.

I turn on my notifications. If anything else comes up, we'll know. I follow my father and Liam for dinner. Before turning in for bed, I check to see if Esmarie's location has stopped, and to make sure my system hasn't flagged anything new. Disappointment is heavy; knowing she is still moving at a rapid pace, we can't go to her without knowing her destination. All I can do is get some rest and hope nothing else comes up to delay me from getting my girl back.

CHAPTER 8

ESMARIE

Once all the men left us alone to settle in for the night, it didn't take long for the girls to start murmuring. They took turns sharing their names and stories of how they ended up here. Most of them were just at the wrong place at the wrong time, and taken off the street. Others were there because they trusted the wrong person. The same betrayal flashing in the eyes I could see was festering in my core. Where they seemed defeated by the betrayal, I used mine to fuel my anger.

I stayed silent, unable to formulate words to describe the betrayal I've pieced together. One question is niggling at my mind: Why? One by one, I listened in solidarity, offering my silent support to the girls I could reach in the cells neighboring mine. While there is a solid metal barrier between us, there is a small gap at the bottom that is large enough for us to slip our hands through.

After that first night, the men returned and beat us into silence. By the third night, we were rendered silent. Part of me regrets not sharing when I had the chance. What if I die here and no one knows my story? I mean, Baldie and presumably Tatum know, but Jasper took care of Baldie. That first night was the night our nightmare truly began. Throughout the night, I heard the whimpers and cries of the other girls as men entered their cells like a revolving door.

Jasper remained at the end of the hallway, closest to me. He remained in my line of sight throughout the whole night. I have an inkling it was so that I knew he wasn't a part of the brutal raping happening. Yet, not once did he look my way. His stoic face was void of emotion as if he was blocking out everything happening around us. I sat awake the entire night, curled in on myself, waiting for my turn. Every man that passed my cell snarled at me, but they never entered. My turn never came. Maybe they're tired and waiting to recuperate. I'd have to be delusional to think I could leave here unscathed.

Sweat and grime cling to me. The stench is becoming unbearable. The men assaulting the girls must not have been able to stomach it any longer. One by one, they escort the girls from their cells, up the stairs. Jasper is the one who escorts me from my cell, leading me past the metal door. He scans his fingerprint before he can open it. He helps me up the stairs and led me through a labyrinth of hallways until we finally stop at a room. I've never been so ecstatic to see a toilet. Other than that, there's nothing other than a drain in the tiled floor. Two other men quickly enter behind Jasper and me. He places a comforting hand on my shoulder before slowly unzipping my dress. Icy panic chills me to my bones. Maybe it's finally my turn, and Jasper will have the honor. Of all the men, I suspect he would be the gentlest.

Cool air pricks my skin as my dress falls in a heap on the floor. Strong arms brace under my armpits as Jasper lifts me from the bundle, depositing me a few feet over. Walking back to my dress, he hangs it over both his arms to prevent it from getting dirtier. It's a useless but kind gesture. He turns his back to me as one of the other men drags me further into the room. He gives me the chance to use the toilet, and I do so shamelessly. A toilet is better than the bucket left for us in our cells.

Before my legs can fully extend to take my weight, I'm dragged toward the drain. The third guy approaches with a hose in his hand. Where it came from, I'm not sure. I don't have the opportunity to figure it out before I'm being pelted with icy water. I splutter as the stream moves from my head, down my body.

When the hose halts its assault, I'm halfheartedly patted down with a towel. Jasper's knuckles are white, his jaw pulsing, before he releases my dress, helping me back into it.

Without a word, he tosses me over his shoulder, storming back to my cell. When he brings me down from his shoulder, he lets my body drag down his own more than necessary. Our eyes connect. My cheeks heat as I glide over the noticeable bulge. He seems genuinely shocked at his body's reaction. He stares down, jaw wide open, at the evidence of his desire for a moment before hurriedly readjusting himself. Wide-eyed, I can see his pupils are blown. He avoids my gaze as he huffs out a cough, hastily exiting the basement.

***

Time here is inconsequential. My days in captivity are gauged by when I sleep. Ever since I found a pebble, I've been using it to track my time in captivity. Tally marks litter the walls. Slowly, I'm losing my grip on reality. Am I really so undesirable that the sex traffickers don't want to touch me? To further break our sanity, the lights remain barely dimmed. There is no indication of whether it's night or day. Meals become infrequent.

After what I can only guess were three nights of waking to any subtle noise, I suspect someone slipped something into my food or water. For the first time since arriving here, I slept peacefully throughout my night.

Clearly, I'm going certifiably insane. I dream of phantom touches and familiar honey eyes. I never wake up sore or bleeding, so I don't think I'm being raped like the other girls. I do, however, wake up with a wet mess between my legs. My thighs press together in shame when I wake. I wonder how it would feel to have the scruff peppering Jasper's jaw rub along my inner thighs. Imagining his eyes peering up at me as his tongue plunges into my pussy only makes me wetter.

Hunger pains have become a familiar friend of mine. When the men start murmuring about auctions, we get fed more, with less frequent beatings. It's not long before the girls are hauled away, replaced by a new lot of prisoners. The hunger is quick to return. Slowly, it ebbs away, just like the girls eventually do. With each trip escorted to the bathing room, I notice fewer girls in the cells. Whether they are being sold off outside the auctions or dying is inconclusive. For their sake, I hope it's the latter. Whatever fate awaits us outside these cells will be much worse than our current predicament.

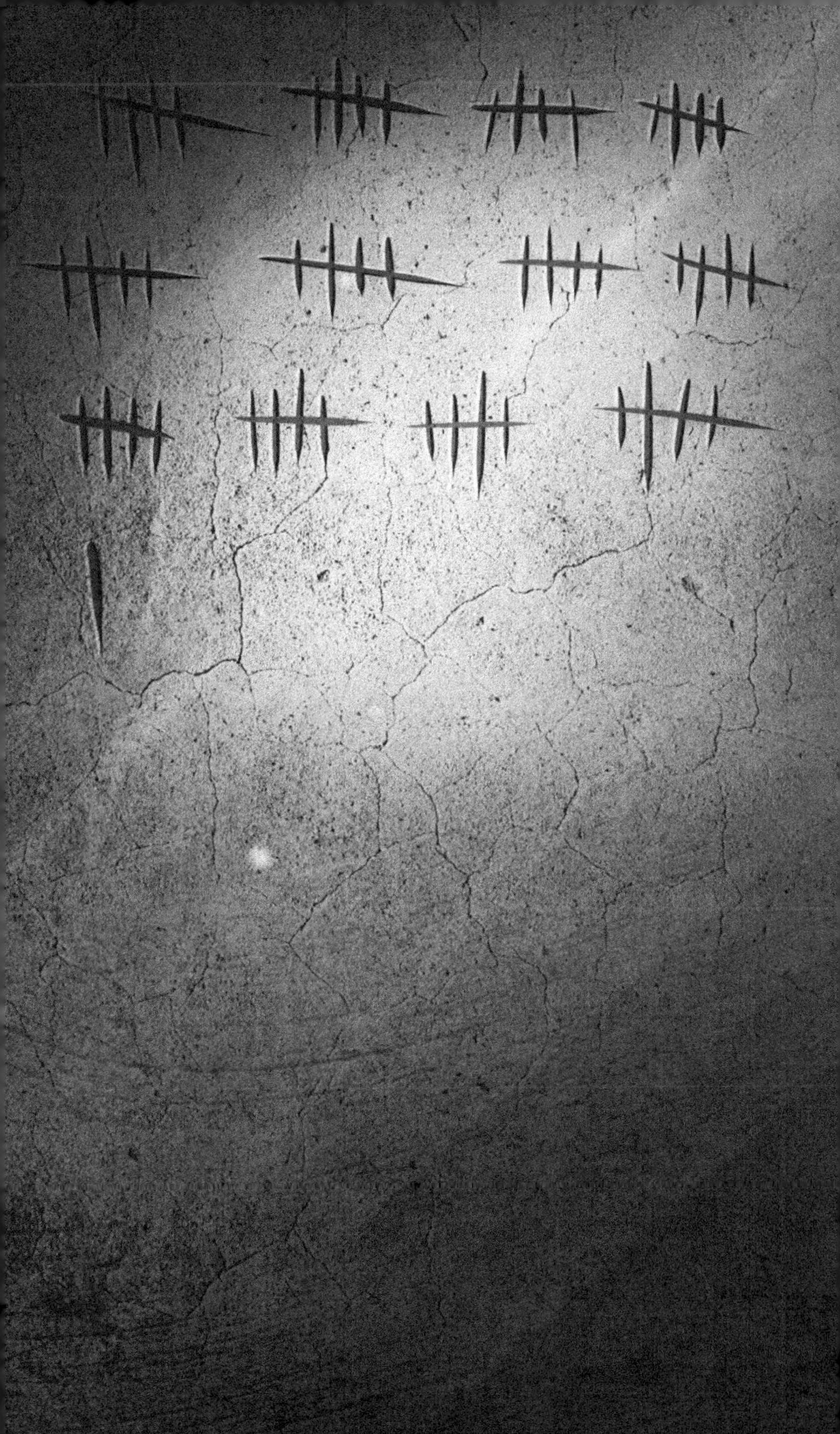

CHAPTER 9

JASPER

It's been over four months since my little hellion was handed over. Her dress hangs off her frame. One night, when she was out cold, I snuck into her cell, adding some snap fasteners. It was the most logical choice given my sewing skills are nonexistent.

By some miracle, Sylvester gave the order to leave her alone that first night. His orders were explicit; she is to be left alone and not broken in like the other girls. His request should've been the first red flag. The delusional part of my brain continues to convince me it's because she prevented him from having to pay out Bruce and having to deal with him any further. Why else would she have remained my prisoner through four auctions?

In all honesty, I don't know what I would do if anyone dared to touch her. She's branded herself onto my soul. My obsession with her flows like lava through my veins. Just because she's not being physically or sexually abused, doesn't mean she's not racking up trauma. Hers just comes in the form of hearing the cries of the other girls as they're brutalized, not knowing if or when it'll be her turn. She does nothing but watch as each new lot of girls is brought in, broken, and auctioned off.

With each day, and every girl sold, my time with my little hellion dwindles. A wild kind of desperation consumes me at the thought of her leaving the little protection I provide her. Once she's sold and handed off to her new handler, she'll be lost forever. There will be nothing I can do to find her.

She is my favorite obsession. Not once has my cock reacted so viscerally to someone before. After her first spray down, I was just as surprised as she was that I had a raging hard-on for her. What she probably doesn't know is that brief contact she made on my cock sent me over the edge. I came in my pants like a fucking adolescent. I was horrified and disgusted with myself, so I ran away like a coward.

Since that day, I've been unable to control myself, and I creep into her cell every night. I wait to sneak in until the sedatives I slip into her dinner knock her out cold. It started out innocent; I just needed to be close to her. I'd just slip in behind her and hold her. Having her in my arms was enough. As my curiosity and obsession grow, so does my boldness in touching her.

It was only a week before I needed more. Unable to resist myself any longer, I cup her sex as I hold her. As if she knows I'm here, her perfect pussy weeps ever so slightly onto my fingers. Every fiber of my being wants to slip a finger inside her wetness, but I resist. Once it's time for me to sneak out, I lick my finger clean while entranced by the rise and fall of her chest.

Her taste is the most potent ambrosia. I need more. So, I patiently wait out the day. By the time I'm sprinkling crushed sedatives into her dinner, I'm already hard. I act as nonchalant as I can as I wait for her eyelids to droop. As soon as she's out, I'm waiting for the last prisoner to fall asleep. Maybe I should drug all the girls so I wouldn't have to wait so long.

Creeping into my little hellion's cell, I quickly slide in behind her. As lust consumes me as I cup her pussy, I contemplate my next move. Surely, one finger wouldn't hurt. Testing the waters, I massage her clit with my thumb. When she lets out a soft moan, I extend my middle finger to dip into her pussy. That's enough to catapult me off the edge, and I'm coming in my pants. I effortlessly coax an orgasm from her. As her pussy spasms around my digit, I collect her juices in the palm of my hand. I greedily lick that shit up.

A small inkling of guilt worms its way into my consciousness for violating her. My sick obsession quickly squashes that nonsense. Observing her body language like I do every morning, she shows no signs of distress upon waking up with a mess between her thighs. When her eyes connect with mine, her breath hitches as she clamps her thighs together. It takes everything in me to remain in my seat when she bites her bottom lip and her cheeks flame.

No matter how much I want to, I refuse to take it any further with her. When I fuck her, she'll be awake and willing. There is no doubt in my mind that sinking into her will be my undoing. She would never escape me.

*****

Sylvester requesting my presence is not out of the ordinary, but certainly unwanted. For one, he's pulling me away from my little hellion. Now, if he knows I've been sneaking into her cell at night, I'm fucked.

My knuckles rasp on the solid oak door twice before he calls for me to enter. I slip into the office like a phantom, locking down all emotions. No need to make him suspicious if he isn't already aware of my nightly activities. I give him a respectful nod in greeting, not wasting our time with meaningless greetings.

"I just need to verify that my order for the little offering is still being maintained," he prods.

My mind flips through which girl he's referring to as an offering, trying to find an outcome that doesn't put my little hellion at the forefront of this summoning. Yet, there's only one captive he's ordered not to be broken in.

"Your word is law, Boss. The girl has not been raped or beaten since arriving," I confirm, not allowing any fluctuation in my tone. Sounding bored is the best way to stop my suspicions from creeping through.

"Good. Mr. Avanzo's quite particular. He'll be ready for her delivery at the end of the month. He's been waiting for his next doll long enough."

The blood in my veins freezes along with every muscle in my body. Ago Avanzo is one of Sylvester's biggest clients. His name is a curse within the cells. His victims are lulled into a false sense of security here. He takes pleasure in being the one to personally break in his toys.

"I'll increase her provisions immediately," I rush out, already knowing the drill when it comes to Ago.

I'm promptly excused. I think about Ago, and my little hellion's looming demise as I make my way back to her. Fuck, how did I not realize she was being prepped to be his next doll?

Ago Avanzo's dolls never last more than a month or two before he's purchasing another. He has a reputation for mutilation and cannibalism. Once he breaks them in, their true fight for survival begins. He cuts the girls up, cooking their flesh in front of them. If they want to eat, their only option is to eat themselves at his hand. I'd assume it was all hearsay, exasperations of the truth, if I didn't hear the admissions straight from his own slimy lips.

The gleam in his eyes when he talks about fucking their corpses does nothing to hide his depravity. When they pass, he dedicates himself to filling them with as much of his seed as possible.

When he's bored with one hole, he's onto the next. Various other holes are made for him to fill, claiming it helps "tenderize the meat." Before they can start rotting away, he butchers what's left of them, saving them to eat later. He made Sylvester a copy of his "special" cookbook for fucks sake. I've managed to avoid being roped into any further meetings with the monster.

Whispers that INTERPOL have been sniffing around him could account for why we haven't delivered a girl to him for the entirety of my little hellion's stay. It must be a record for him. There's no way his latest victim has lasted this long. It would be hard to purchase sex slaves to torture and eat when your assets being tracked by multiple federal agencies.

While he's quite vocal about his extracurricular activities, one would think that's why they've been on his ass. Nope. According to the news, he has a warrant out for his arrest for tax evasion.

Over my dead body will my little hellion be handed over like a sheep to the slaughter. Right now, I'll make sure she's well fed and taken care of under the guise of compliance to my orders. If the plans swirling around in my mind are going to work, she'll need meat on her bones in order to regain her strength.

Our deaths will be our only escape. We are both aware of this fact. Faking our death is the only logical choice. Since we are hidden away in the mountainous woods, it's not unusual for the soldiers to familiarize ourselves with the terrain. So, when obtaining deliveries, I'll wander around, scoping out the area. No one will question a thing.

Stalking my way through the rows of cells toward my obsession, an unblinking gaze has me halting my pursuit. A wicked grin splays across my lips. She's roughly the same height as my hellion, just a lot worse for wear. Seeing my hellion will just have to wait.

My fingers fly across my burner phone, sending a message through our secure line. I inform the team we're down a girl, and I'm disposing of her before she can stink up the basement any further. Intentionally, I never mention how. I won't be incinerating her, as per protocol. Instead, I carry her out the nearest door, to a little alcove on the side of the mountain. She's so malnourished that she weighs nothing as I carry her through the rough terrain.

Tomorrow, I'll slip something into one of the runners' food that'll make him sick for a few days. With any luck, I'll get the orders to take over his tasks. Then, I'll have an excuse to be in town without having to wait for the next shipment of girls. Mentally, I run through a list of things I'll need to do: rob some houses for clothes and supplies, siphon some gas into canisters from unsuspecting cars, and find a man with my build to join the deceased girl I stashed away.

CHAPTER 10

ESMARIE

Weariness has found a silent home within my bones. Girls have come and gone. Yet, I remain locked away in this cage. I'm lost in the solitude of my thoughts. The clatter of the other girls being delivered their daily provisions is the only thing luring me out of my trance. It's the only thing breaking the mundane silence.

There's no hiding the fact that a second portion gets delivered to my cell. I've never been so thankful to be isolated in the darkness. I can't exactly see the envy burning in their eyes, but I feel it all the same. Whoever is in charge of my meals has worked my stomach up to accepting three provisional meals a day. It only serves to racket up my suspicions and hope simultaneously.

I've caught onto the cycle of when they bring in new girls. It always starts the same. We get fed more, and the abuse halts. The girls get dragged from their cells, only they never return. I remain alone until new girls are brought in to fill the cells.

The stale silence is broken by the worried chatter. Then, the scary men come and beat them into silence. The whispers turn into whimpers. Those whimpers turn into screams as they are brutally raped throughout the night. Yet, with each passing day, I'm left physically unharmed.

My mind is the only thing being damaged. When the men come to deliver their daily dose of pain, I wince each time the shrill cries for help turn mute. Unable to see the past a few cells in front of me, I've still seen enough to know that the sudden silence is more often death being delivered to them through brutal torture. For their sake, I hope it's death and not them being beaten unconscious. At least in death, they won't wake back up to this nightmare and they're free from their suffering.

I'm not sure what divine being has been watching over me, but I'm thankful. Anxiety looms in the back of my mind, waiting for the day my lucky streak ends and the men have their way with me. The only times I've been touched are the gentle caresses I dream of.

But this draconian basement of horrors is not home to any gentleness. If it were, Jasper would help the girls when they plead for someone to save them. So, it's unreasonable to believe the gentle touches bringing me pleasure in the night are nothing more than a fragment of my imagination.

Jasper lingers in my periphery during those nights. When this desolate place first became my home, Jasper's looming presence haunted me. Now, his presence is comforting and his absence fills me with dread. I notice it keenly, given the other men tend to stay away when he's around. When he's gone, they crowd my cell like vultures. Much to my dismay, today's another day that Jasper's seemingly disappeared.

Footsteps thundering down the stairs has my hackles rising. There's nowhere for me to hide, and Jasper isn't here to offer me his twisted brand of protection. Metal batons batter against the bars to my cell as five men stand in front of me.

"Well, if it isn't the little doll left unprotected," one sneers.

"How long do you think the doll will last with its new owner before it's broken? Maybe we should break her in now so she has a fighting chance," another one questions as he unlocks my cell door.

A chorus of laughter erupts. Leaning to peer around them, I meet the wide-eyed stares of the girls across from me. The dim lights they start the girls out with are a luxury before the night vision goggles come out and darkness takes over. Right now, it's a curse because I can see my fear reflected in their eyes. Why are they referring to me as a doll? They usually refer to the other girls as bitches or a slew of other derogatory terms. Doll seems oddly specific.

Acrid body odor wafts toward my nose as they crowd in around me. Pain explodes across my cheek with the first strike of their fists. They take turns hitting and mocking me.

My vision narrows as one eye swells shut. My arms do nothing to protect me against the attack. Curled on the ground, I'm pummeled by the steel in their boots. I gag past the metallic taste flooding my mouth. Greedy hands tug my dress from my body, exposing me to the debris littering the stone floor. Pants quickly litter the floor. Icy air licks at my skin alongside their unwanted groping.

Heavy weight pins my legs to the ground, spread as wide as my ligaments will allow. My breasts are crushed beneath the weight of another man restraining me further. All the men surrounding me fist their tiny cocks, waiting to get off on my suffering. Right as the biggest man kneels between my legs, pumping his cock furiously, footsteps thunder down the stairs. I lay as still as possible praying it's not another man coming to join my torture.

"What the fuck do you all think you're doing? Boss was very clear in his instructions to leave the doll alone!" a familiar voice, angrier than I've heard, booms from the bottom of the stairs.

Jasper stalks into view. I've never seen him so close to the edge of violence. He yanks the man from between my thighs. Without hesitation, he grasps the man's erection. There's a sickening snap, followed by howls of pain echoing through the basement. Not wanting to be the next victim of Jasper's wrath, the men holding me down creep away from me as fast as possible without garnering his vengeful attention.

I suppose I need to figure out who their boss is. I have him to thank for keeping this from happening to me sooner. I thought the man cloaked in violence in front of me was my only guardian in this hell.

Pale faced, the men retreat up the stairs like scolded puppies. I remain motionless, letting the stone floor chill my battered body. Tactical boots come into view as Jasper kneels beside me. Frowning, he examines my discarded dress before tugging off his shirt and dragging it over my head.

Standing, he turns his back to me. "Who knows how to sew?"

Silence lingers in the air. The other girls don't trust that this isn't a trick to beat them if they respond.

"If one of you can fix this dress without trying to harm yourself, I'll provide everyone with extra food and blankets," he bargains.

Soft murmurs start floating around, begging that someone will step up. Jasper waits patiently until someone reluctantly agrees. Warmth envelops me as I'm swept up off the ground. Effortlessly, Jasper carries me through the locked door and up the stairs. I recognize the path leading us toward the room they spray us down in.

Tension leaves my shoulders as he continues sauntering past it. We turn down a few more hallways before stopping in front of a door. Any sane person would be scared being carted into an unfamiliar area, but I'm no longer sane. Jasper did just save me from being raped, after all.

One arm holds me as he uses the other to push the door open, exposing a quaint bedroom. It's bare, with only a small cot and a bedside table. Slowly, I'm lowered to the cot. It feels luxurious after sleeping on the ground. Jasper disappears behind a door. Running water is soon accompanied by the aroma of lavender.

I don't realize I've dozed off until my eyelids flutter open when strong arms encircle me once more. Taking in the steaming bath waiting for me, hot tears flow down my cheeks. Slowly, Jasper lowers me until my toes dip into the water. Crystals crunch beneath me from the undissolved Epsom salts.

Bracing myself on his corded forearms, I lower myself until I'm submerged in the warm water, uncaring that I'm drenching the shirt he dressed me in. Pulling my knee up, I band my arms around them in a protective embrace. Using a cup, he gently pours the warm water over my hair and back.

"Is it all right if I touch you to wash your hair?" he softly asks.

With my vocal cords long forgotten, I offer a single nod. Working in small sections, he wordlessly does his best to comb out my hair with surprising tenderness, occasionally spritzing my hair. Jasper works so long, he partially drains the chilled water to refill the tub with fresh steaming water twice before he even lathers my head with shampoo. He uses a cup to rinse the suds away, making sure to keep the water out of my ears and face.

After slathering the conditioner on, his fingers hover over my skin in a moment of hesitation. Mechanically, he scrubs my exposed skin with a washcloth. He goes at detangling my rat's nest once more as the water swirls down the drain. He uses the warm water pouring from the faucet to rinse away the last of the product.

"I'm going to step out and deliver the sewing supplies. Can I trust that you won't do anything stupid while I'm gone?" he asks in a rough whisper.

I wait until his eyes lock on mine before nodding. He needs to see the promise in my eyes. Being in this room has been a dream. I wouldn't risk cutting whatever this is short.

The muscles in his jaw flex as he ghosts his finger over my shattered cheekbone. Flinching in pain, I debate on asking him to bring me some ice to reduce the swelling. Opening my eyes, I catch the tail end of his hasty retreat.

Allowing the water to soothe my muscles for a little longer, I give myself a few minutes to simply relax. When the last of the water is drained away, I peel off the wet T-shirt. I quickly scrub the areas Jasper dutifully avoided, jumping at the noise of water thundering out.

Eyeing the towel left on the counter, I climb out of the bathtub. Soft cotton envelops me as I wrap it around myself. The oversized linen dwarfs me, hanging from around my shoulders and drooping to my knees.

My fingers wrap around the doorknob, hoping he didn't lock me in this bathroom. Unlocked, I sneak into the bedroom hoping I can lie back down in the cot while I'm here. Laid out waiting for me, is a fresh T-shirt and sweatpants. I slip into them before climbing beneath the lightweight comforter.

Santal and citrus surrounds me. I bury my nose into the shirt where the intoxicating aroma is more potent. The door creaks open and I blush at being caught.

A smirk crosses his lips, but he says nothing. Rather, he glides into the room with a tray in hand. Joining me on the bed, he offers me an artfully crafted sandwich and an ice pack. Together, we eat in silence. My bites are small, not wanting this meal to be over, or make me sick.

"Come on, little hellion. I need to take you back now," Jasper whispers while lifting me back into his arms.

I make no move to put up a fight, too focused on holding the ice to my swollen eye. I'm resigned to my fate, I'm not delusional enough to think I'd be staying in this room.

Waiting for me in my cell is my dress. The usual grogginess that accompanies me when I eat my last meal of the day never comes. Maybe it's because Jasper brought me the food himself, ensuring it wasn't tampered with. I shouldn't be so disappointed that it wasn't him drugging my food, but it bothers me nonetheless. Not because it was someone else drugging me, but because I was hoping he was the reason I wake up hot and bothered after every suspiciously deep sleep.

Not wanting him to see my tears, I give him my back. On shaky legs, I stumble toward my dress. It's covered in filth and no longer the pristine ivory. The clank of the iron door locking me in my cell echoes through the unnaturally silent basement.

Turning around, I see him staring at me through the iron bars separating us. His eyes flicker toward the lock briefly before meeting my gaze once more. Swiftly, he leaves like a predator in the night.

I sit in the corner of my cell, more alert than ever. I feel refreshed and for once, hunger evades me. I replay in my mind how he cared for me in that room. Everything plays on a loop, up to the point of him locking me back in here.

My spine straightens. Yes, he shut the door to the cell, but I don't recall hearing the click of the lock engaging. Did he forget? Was he trying to communicate that to me when he stared at me and glanced at the lock?

Hope blooms in my stomach. This may be my only chance to escape this hell hole. I'll wait a little longer to make sure the coast is clear, ensuring he's not coming back. Then, I'll run like hell. My life depends on it.

CHAPTER 11

BECKETT

Not having access to a live feed of Esmarie is the worst type of torture. I'm a fiend, desperate for my next glimpse of her. Not having cameras to watch her through is disheartening. All I'm left with are the recorded tapes I've saved.

When Esmarie first moved into her apartment, I knew I had the opportunity I've been waiting for. William kept her on a tight leash. There was no chance in hell I would be able to slip into his home to place cameras in Esmarie's bedroom. The first weekend William called her home, I abandoned all responsibilities under the guise of having the stomach flu in order to take full advantage of the opportunity of having unbridled access to watch Esmarie at all times.

Adrenaline surges through me as I reminisce how I rushed to Montreal. I abused my training, using my honed skills to break into her empty apartment and place as many cameras I needed to quell my sick urge.

Having high quality footage of her from every inch of her apartment provided a potent hit of dopamine that was unattainable by tracking her through fuzzy, low quality traffic and security cameras.

Esmarie is something else. I learned a few key things very quickly. She loved being nude within the confines of her home. That apartment was her safe place. All the tension from carrying around William's expectations melted away the moment the door clicked shut behind her. Most importantly, Esmarie was curious about exploring her body and what brought her the most pleasure.

It's no surprise that William wanted Esmarie to remain pure. He and Anastasia did a wondrous job keeping boys away from her, directing all male attention toward Anastasia. Instead of Esmarie rebelling and sneaking around behind their backs, it bred insecurity so deep that she avoided guys entirely. Their blatant dismissal of the diamond in front of them for her easier sister only festered old wounds.

The way Esmarie hid while she pleasured herself, it was apparent that she found the task shameful; much to my dismay. Relying heavily on my imagination, I touched myself alongside her each night. Not once did I see evidence that she was using a toy, but rather her nimble fingers to draw out the delicious whimpers that would float through my speakers.

Resorting to my baser instincts, I uploaded my favorite videos of Esmarie sleeping on my phone. Knowing she's naked, getting nothing more than a glimpse of the side of her bare breast is a stronger aphrodisiac than if she were laid out bare. I've seen her naked plenty, but it's something else entirely to undress her with my imagination alone in those moments she lies utterly vulnerable.

My nightly routine is the same as always. In the ambiguity of darkness, I give myself over to my desires. Mechanically, I select my favorite video of Esmarie. Laying my phone on my mattress beneath me, I pull my pants past my hips allowing my erection to spring free.

Hovering over the screen I imagine she's lying under me with her perfect pussy exposed as an offering. I fuck my fist as I watch her sleep, focusing on the way she cups her breast and the seductive parting of her pillowy lips. I fantasize about how addictive it would be to hold the weight of her plump breasts in my hands, how it would feel to have her lips gasping against mine as I please her.

Tightening my grip, I thrust into my fist faster. Pleasure licks up my spine, causing me to bite my lip in an attempt to muffle my moans. The walls here are thin, and no one needs to know what happens between Esmarie and me when the lights are off.

Even though I've watched this particular video thousands of times, it's still a surprise when she jerks in her sleep. The sudden movement jolts the floral duvet enough to expose pert nipples. It gets me every. Single. Time.

Cum spurts from my cock, coating Esmarie. Ignoring my mess, I zoom in on her face imagining she's here with me. There's a primal desire to both fill and cover her in my seed. My cock twitches in my fist and I groan as I continue stroking my sensitive shaft.

My fantasies shatter as the ringtone for Mr. Beaumont's emergency team cuts through my otherwise silent room. I cringe seeing my release now coating my phone screen. Quickly, I wipe the glass off the best I can before pressing the sticky phone to my ear.

"We need everyone back at headquarters. NOW," Decker, the head of Mr. Beaumont's personal security team commands before hanging up. His calculated tone leaves no room for argument.

We all know what this means. Rescuing Esmarie is going to have to wait. I know it's not what Emmett would want, but he's the boss; his safety is our main priority. He trusts Decker enough to make these calls, which means we have no choice but to obey.

We can no longer stay in the safe house. I log into the app connected to Esmarie's tracker as I prepare to head back to headquarters. It takes longer than normal to log in, but I think nothing of it as I slip my phone back in my pocket as I pack up to leave.

Maintaining Mr. Beaumont's cyber defenses while trying to flush out the mole from half-way across the country is no longer feasible. The threats against Mr. Beaumont are no longer just about taking over his empire. BeauCrest demands nothing but unwavering loyalty, and that loyalty has been broken. The initial financial threats have morphed into death threats.

The violent nature of the threats have escalated far too quickly, and they certainly can't be ignored. For Decker, this means there is no hesitation in pulling the plug on Mr. Beaumont's daughter's rescue. This is a code red, requiring all hands-on deck back at headquarters. It's clear that we have at least one mole within our ranks.

***

The first month was spent conducting interrogations and listening in on whispers. Working back at headquarters made it much easier to flush out the mole. Slowly, we pieced together the puzzle of who was disloyal amongst us. Our sights narrowed on three men. They signed their death certificates the moment they decided to double cross Mr. Beaumont.

The second month was spent tracking down each of the moles without tipping them off that we were onto them. The first mole we uncovered wasn't much of a surprise. He was recruited less than a year ago. That, coupled with the fact his mother was going through an experimental chemo treatment, made him easily susceptible to bribes.

The second mole was a surprise that had us revamping all of our security measures. He was an agent who had been working directly under Decker for years. Decker personally vetted him for his team, so his trust was never questioned.

He must have caught word of our manhunt, because the night we came for him, he tried to escape into the night. Unfortunately for him, he was unaware of the subdermal tracker placed during his initial physical. He also left behind his shredded evidence.

After days of piecing together the ribbons of the world's worst puzzle, we made the first breakthrough of who was behind all the threats. Once we captured the rogue agent and presented him the taped up files he tried to dispose of, he sang like a canary.

The final mole behind everything was the hardest to come to terms with. I've never seen Mr. Beaumont so stricken. None other than William Kensington—his half-brother—was the main culprit. We knew that Anastasia and Tatum were trying to access Esmarie's trust, but we thought greed was their only motivation. It was a huge misstep on our part to not have considered that William was the one who tipped them off about her trust in the first place. We knew of Bruce's involvement, but after we found his body with a bullet hole in between his eyes, we wrote it off under the assumption we already uncovered all the facts, and he was a loose end William tied up.

As the secrets continued to unravel, they painted a picture of bitter jealousy. Since William had a different father, he was excluded from the family business. He felt he was entitled to everything the Beaumont legacy built.

William had no interest in being involved with the business, he just wanted the money and prestige that came hand in hand with being its leader. William conned Tatum Carter into marrying Esmarie and blackmailed Bruce into aiding Anastasia after she found out Esmarie wasn't really his daughter and would be able to access the billions waiting for her when she turned twenty-six.

Mr. Beaumont trusted his half-brother to raise and protect his daughter all these years. Now, finding Esmarie is even more crucial. Throughout all of this, Liam was tasked with monitoring Esmarie's movements throughout the day once he was cleared. Not wanting anything to do with the violence and chaos, he quickly obliged the orders allowing him to hide behind his screen. Back in his comfort zone, he took his duties seriously, watching the red dot indicating Esmarie like a hawk.

It wasn't long before Liam reported that Esmarie's tracker was being glitchy. Within days, we were all locked out. William must've hired a highly skilled hacker to be able to hack into the app we created solely for Esmarie's tracker. Mr. Beaumont looped in our highest ranking hackers to help get us back in.

If someone knew of Esmarie's identity, and had access to her location, it could be disastrous. For an entire torturous month, we were in the dark. We managed to track down the IP address of the hacker. If we weren't so furious with him for putting Esmarie's safety in jeopardy, then Mr. Beaumont may have considered recruiting him.

As we prepare for our new operation, Mr. Beaumont paces behind his desk. His turmoil is etched clearly across his face. I can't fathom the guilt he must be feeling. He thought he could trust his brother, and that sending Esmarie away would keep her safe from his enemies. He didn't want his precious daughter meeting the same fate as his beloved wife. With his biggest enemy being his brother, maybe she would have been safer by his side this whole time.

"You know your orders. Get my daughter back. I will not risk her safety any longer. We need to be prepared for the worst. Take medical with you. Decker, I need you to outline an intensive combat program for her. You'll train her personally. I need to know she can defend herself if anything like this arises again." Mr. Beaumont's voice remains steely and as well composed as ever.

Finally, the moment I've been waiting for has arrived. With our orders, we board the private jet. With one last confirmation from Liam that Esmarie's in Albania, something in me settles knowing we are on our way.

It'll take a little over half a day to reach our destination. Due to the mountainous terrain her location is pinging in, we opted for half of the team to parachute from the jet in order to get to her as quickly as possible while the others land with the jet and wait for us in the nearest town.

Me, along with the militia team, will be the ones extracting her. Since I have the tactical skills to both track Esmarie and combat skills, I will lead our best soldiers to her. We are approaching this with guns blazing since we have no idea how many assailants will be waiting for us.

While most of the team rests for the remaining six hours of the flight, Liam has dutifully stayed awake with his eyes glued to the screen. I allowed myself an hour of shut eye before nerves got the best of me. Offering Liam a break instead, I've been staring at the unmoving flashing red dot for an hour when it began to move.

Blinking, I cease breathing. making sure my mind wasn't just playing tricks on me. The red dot moved. Esmarie is moving. Dread fills my stomach like lead. Immediately, I wake Liam. His jaw drops, looking at me wide eyed waiting for me to confirm what this means.

"Go inform the pilot the target is on the move." I track her movement along the screen long enough to confirm she is not traveling a substantial distance to indicate she is in a vehicle. Turning back to an anxious Liam, I add, "For now, we're good to proceed to the original coordinates. We'll reconvene when we're closer."

Decker, Liam, and I huddle around my screen watching Esmarie travel mile after mile. She must be running through the wilderness. Just under two hours later, Esmarie's movement halts. She is approximately five miles away from the one-mile radius she stayed within the confines in all this time.

Panic has me in a chokehold. Realistically, she must be resting. But what if she has collapsed from exhaustion, or worse, her captors found and killed her? Liam softly assures me it's not worth letting the panic consume me when there is nothing we can do while in the air. Common sense tells me he's right, but my mind is filled with worst case scenarios. Failure and helplessness consume me as I'm frozen in my seat, praying the little red dot will resume its movement once more.

CHAPTER 12

JASPER

My plan is working. Turns out, my little hellion still has some fight left in her. My cock grows hard knowing she didn't make me wait long. Soft footsteps padding along the wooden stairs mark her ascension. While she was pretending to sleep, I snuck back down to the cells and hid in a back corner. Throwing my masks on, I creep out of my hiding spot, making sure my hellion took her gift with her.

Frowning, I see her soiled gown laying where I left it. Tenderly, I fold it tightly, packing it away in my backpack. Whimpers escape from the girls we're leaving behind. They don't know who's behind the mask. I could be here to brutalize them, or I could be coming to serve out punishment for the doll who escaped.

The girls here don't know the significance of the nickname, or that a million years in these cells would be paramount to being Ago's little doll. Over my dead body will my hellion be subjected to that decrepit man's torture. I refuse to admit that true fear struck me when I found out that it was her fate.

It gave me the motivation to do what I have always thought about. Getting the hell out and taking her beautiful soul with me. I refuse to let my hellion become another one of Ago's dolls to be lost to the world forever, without a single trace.

My trap was laid perfectly. I sprayed the walls with my cologne before unlocking the doors to each lower level of the house. All she needs to do is follow my scent. In case that's not enough, I follow close enough behind her that she doesn't notice me, directing her through the maze of hallways with a laser pointer faint enough, she could mistake it for a hallucination.

She easily makes it through the hallways until she slips right out the final door. I knew my scent was irresistible to her. She probably dreamed of it each night and awoke to it lingering on her. It led her like a beacon to a ship.

I watch, transfixed as she tears out of the house at lightning speed, only hesitating when the fresh air hits her like a brick wall. Her hesitation only lasts a moment before she's sprinting into the wilderness, trying to put as much distance between her and that hell hole.

With a smirk on my lips, I give chase. I can't say I feel guilty for this sick game. Her feet must be hurting. The ground is littered with sharp rocks and forest debris.

Before giving into the chase so I can devour her like the true prey that she is, I snap out of my fantasy and corner her. My arms snake out, wrapping around her waist startles her. A leather clad palm swiftly covers her mouth, muffling her cries. Tossing around in my arms, she tries to escape, but to no avail.

"Shhh, my little hellion. I promise I'm not going to hurt you," I coo. "I need you to be quiet for me. Can you do that?"

She pauses her futile attempt to escape to ponder my words. Once I'm sure she won't scream, blowing our cover, I allow my hand to slip away from her lips. I planned our escape in the dead of night to prevent any damage that the jarring sunlight would do to her retinas. After all, she has been locked away in a basement that alternated between dimly lit and pitch black for months.

Deciding to give her torn up feet a reprieve, I cradle her in my arms. My legs carry us swiftly through the trees to our destination. When I was preparing for our escape, I overheard that some of the townsfolk were really big into doomsday prepping. It's not widely known information, but with the right motivation, they quickly disclosed a few of their hidden bunker locations.

Our safe haven is only ten miles away. As luck would have it, our doppelgangers are hidden away in a cave along the way. We'll have to make a pitstop. When Sylvester's men eventually come after us, they'll track us right where I want them. I'll just have to hide our tracks when we leave the alcove.

While my little hellion remains silent, I feel her gaze piercing through my mask. I wonder if she knows it's me and that's why she's not fighting me. Once we reach the alcove, I know we don't have much time before the alarm will be sounded. At the first rays of sunlight, they'll be hunting us like bloodhounds.

"I'm going to set you down. I need you to stay put and not run away. I just need to do something quick and grab some supplies I've hidden for us."

As I step away from her, I prepare myself. Watching, I wait to see if she decides to make a run for it. When it seems like she's catering to my commands, I retreat further into the alcove without turning my back to her.

The closer I get to the bodies, the thicker the putrid stench of their decaying bodies becomes. Not wanting to get any closer, I gag back bile. I make quick work of dousing them in kerosene, leading a trail a safe distance away from them. Striking a match, I flick it toward the puddle before me. Flames dance their way to the rotting corpses. As their remains ignite, I grab the supplies and sprint toward the entrance. Scooping my hellion back up, I take us further into the woods and closer to our salvation.

Fighting against exhaustion, I power on carrying my little hellion to the underground bunker. It would have been easier if I made her run alongside me, or at least walked with her in my arms, but the faster we get away, the safer we are.

Part of my preparation was looping a shoelace on a branch marking each mile to our hideout. I've been snagging them as

I go. If needed, I can use them as restraints. Oh, how I wish I could see the foot soldiers' frustration as they wake to find their boots lace less.

Gathering the tenth lace, a newfound burst of energy flows through me. Exerting myself harder, I ignore the burn in my legs. Scanning the ground, I look for the slight disruption in the vegetation. Admittedly, the bunker is well camouflaged, and if you didn't know what you were looking for, you'd never find it.

Dawn is breaking over the horizon, providing faint lighting. Nerves crash over me like waves, knowing the countdown has truly begun. I need to find the bunker. Now. Sweat drips into my eyes, blurring my already limited vision.

At last, I see the slight indent of the forest floor where the vegetation is imperceptibly more vibrant. Setting Esmarie on the damp ground, she startles awake. Lifting a finger to my lips, she understands I need her to be quiet. Some part of me knows she needs comfort. I also don't want to let her go completely. So, I grasp one of her tiny hands in mine, as I use my dominant one to open the bunker.

With a soft click, the door springs open a few inches, allowing me to pull it up the rest of the way. My hellions eyes are as wide as saucers, looking fearfully into the black abyss below.

"I need you to climb down first. I promise there's nothing down there that'll hurt you. We need to hide, and this bunker is the safest place for us," I encourage her.

Defiance flickers behind her hazel eyes. Fumbling through my bag, I find a flashlight and carelessly flick it on. She winces at the light. Shit, that probably burned her retinas. She's been in nothing but darkness during her captivity, it's part of their disorientation.

Shoving the flashlight under my shirt, I direct the muted light into the bunker below. Some of the tension leaves her shoulders once she sees there is no ambush waiting for her. Gingerly, she crawls her way to the edge and places a foot on the first rung of the ladder.

Painstakingly slow, my little hellion descends into the bunker. Once she's a few steps away from the entrance, I swiftly make my way down, securing the door closed behind me. The immense relief of the weight being lifted from my shoulders is immediate. We made it.

The bunker isn't much. It's no bigger than the cargo container my little hellion was delivered to me in. The metal walls do nothing to provide warmth or comfort. Along the back wall is a cabinet of dry goods and supplies. Two murphy beds are built into the side walls. The beds are threadbare and more of a bedroll than a cot, but they are better than nothing. To the back is a small door leading to a makeshift bathroom.

Lighting a lamp, I place it in the furthest corner of the bathroom. Shutting the door controls the amount of light shining through, leaving just enough for us to be able to see. My hellion's eyes need to work up a tolerance. Pulling down one of the beds, I sweep my arm out, offering it to my hellion before focusing on the other bed.

Creaking metal springs reverberates through the silence as she crawls onto the bed. I slump onto my bed, content to study her. Her mouth seems to be moving, but no sound escapes her lips. Frowning, I try to recount if she screamed to the point her vocal cords would have been damaged. When I picked her up from the cargo train, she talked just fine, demanding her handler not gain anything from her demise. Perhaps it's just a trauma response.

"Say that again?" I ask, my eyes not straying from her lips for a second. I've obtained a variety of skills throughout my time working for Sylvester. Lip reading being the most important one right now.

How long do we have to stay here? she soundlessly asks.

"We have a month of rations here, but I hope we can relocate before we get close to running out. I don't want to keep you caged up here longer than necessary."

Appeased, she nods. Her frustration of not being able to communicate melts away as she realizes if my eyes are on her, I can understand her without her making a sound. Springing off the bed, she launches herself at me. For a brief moment, I think she may be coming to attack me. My training kicks in and I launch to my feet, preparing to meet the attack head on. Instead, frail arms latch around my waist, as she burrows her face in my chest. I think she's hugging me. Hiccupping sobs have her jerking against me. Hot tears seep through my cotton shirt.

When I try to pull her off me, she clings on harder. Trying once more, I pry her away enough to sit and cradle her in my lap. Her head finds a resting place in the crook of my neck. Slowly, her sobs turn to whimpers as her body is drained of its strength.

My little hellion cries herself to sleep in my arms, clutching onto me like I'm her last salvation. Laying us down, I hold her close as I, too, drift to sleep.

CHAPTER 13

ESMARIE

Warm breaths puff against my back as strong arms pull me into a hard chest. My heart rate accelerates, not recognizing my surroundings before last night's events play back in my mind.

On the pillow in front of me lies the skull mask and balaclava. Faint traces of santal and citrus linger on the linen encasing me. Was it really Jasper who helped me escape? Slowly, I twist in his arms, doing my best not to disrupt the man behind me. I need to see his face. I've only been so compliant because I suspected it was Jasper hiding behind the mask in the woods.

Honey eyes greet me when I manage to wiggle my way around. My relief is palpable as I take in the man before me. Jasper. I blink away the pressure growing behind my eyes, overwhelmed with the barrage of emotions. Mortification overwhelms me as memories of my actions last night filter in. I don't want to cry in front of him again.

Something long and hard presses against my leg. Realization hits, and my cheeks flame. Jasper dutifully ignores his erection, remaining perfectly still.

"Morning, little hellion. Did you sleep all right?" he quietly asks.

His eyes search for a reaction to waking in his arms, his concern evident. Guilt pinches his features, worrying he crossed a line by holding me throughout the night. Little does he know his arms are the only thing holding me together.

When I try to alleviate his nerves, nothing more than a squeak passes my lips. I hate the pitying look he gives me. Why can't I make the words come out?

"Let's get you some food," he offers instead.

Icy air replaces his comforting heat as he leaves me alone in the tiny bed. No wonder he held me so close; I'm precariously close to hanging off the edge. Shivers rack my body, so I pull the blanket closer around me.

Jasper rummages around before returning with some bread and an opened can of peaches.

"Sorry. It's not much, but it's still better than what you were getting in the cell. I figured this would be easier on your stomach than the MRE's."

I nod my thanks. My eyes roll to the back of my skull as the first chunk of the juicy fruit lands on my tongue. Meals in captivity would be considered good if it wasn't mushy or something other than stale bread. The bread alone is a pillowy luxury.

Jasper watches me eat with an easy-going smile. He quickly devours his own can of peaches and bread. Doesn't he need more than that? Someone of his size can't possibly survive off the same portions as me.

Not wanting to be sick, I take my time, savoring my breakfast. Content to bask in the silence, I see Jasper in a whole new light. I thought he was handsome when I met him. Examining him now, his honey eyes glow like amber. The faintest hint of stubble speckles his sharp jawline.

This gorgeous yet strong man has been my guardian angel. He kept me sane while I was trapped in my cell. He's saved me once more, by helping me escape. I can't help but wonder if it's me he wanted to save, or if he was trying to run away himself and I was a convenient tagalong he found in the woods.

You helped me escape, didn't you? I mouth my question, desperately needing the answer.

Holding my breath waiting for the truth, he studies me before responding. He shatters my doubts with one single word. "Yes."

Why? I try to ask once he focuses on my lips.

Jasper deliberates, trying to figure out how much he should divulge. Honestly, I don't care what his answer is as long as it doesn't involve me being sold again; or him murdering me.

"You've become somewhat of an obsession of mine. I couldn't stand you being there, and they were preparing to sell you to a very bad man. I couldn't let that happen," he admits.

If they find you, won't they kill you? Why risk helping me?

"They would, without hesitation. But they'll have to find us first, and I don't intend on that happening. It's my escape just as much as yours."

When I just stare at him, waiting for him to say more, he waits a beat before continuing. "I got tangled up in my brother's mistakes. When he died and could no longer repay his debts, it became my burden. I hate everything that they are. I can't tell you how many bullet holes it took for me to be left alone to simply be on guard duty. I wanted out and was prepared to do so by any means necessary. Your arrival made me want to get out without ending up in a body bag," Jasper whispers, his eyes refusing to meet mine.

His shame for his involvement is clear. Lingering resentment for his brother should be concerning. Remembering Anastasia and my husband's betrayal has me softening in understanding. His shame lies in his involvement and being forced to watch us be tortured and wither away. Jasper fidgets, desperate for a subject change.

"Um, I did a little research on how to help you readjust from the light deprivation. I got an ultraviolet light lamp. We'll start with it dimmed, but we're going to work up to increase the exposure so it's easier for you to acclimate when we leave here. I have sunglasses in case it gets too much. I also got some vitamins to help stabilize your deficiencies."

Heat creeps up my neck. It's such a simple gesture, yet it stirs an avalanche of emotions inside me. I give him a thankful smile. Suddenly, I'm agitated that I can't just get the words to come back so we can have a real conversation that doesn't involve him reading my lips.

Do something for me, please? I mime. Blinded by his thoughtfulness, I've never felt safer.

"Anything," he easily agrees.

Hesitantly climbing onto his lap, I straddle his thighs. Patiently waiting for my request, he arches a brow for me to elaborate.

Fuck me. Please, just fuck me. I want it to be on my own terms while I have the chance. I know if we get caught, I won't be so lucky to be spared the being raped a second time around, I plead.

His nostrils flare, his fingers clamping on my hips. His anger is palpable, but the fear never comes. It's not directed at me. His anger is on my behalf. Jerking my hips so I'm settled on his cock, he crashes his lips to mine in a brutal kiss.

The kiss eases up and I'm entranced by how tenderly his lips entangle with mine. There's no hesitation at the fact I haven't brushed my teeth recently. If it weren't for the glorious bath he snuck me into, the last time toothpaste blessed my mouth was when he brushed my teeth for me during my last spray down. It's been so long since they've been scrubbed clean.

Before my self-consciousness takes over, he pulls me in closer. His erection is solid between my thighs. I instinctively roll my hips against him. We let out a groan at the same time from the delectable sensation. I need more; so much more.

Still dressed in his sweats and T-shirt, he peels his shirt over my head. His own shirt is quick to follow. Ink covers his broad chest and chiseled abs. My fingers glide along his muscles, needing to feel him.

Ridges litter his skin. The ink merely hides the scars. His flinch away from my gentle touch is nearly imperceptible. My hands are drawn away as he flips us. Looking up at him, I see the desire bleeding into his eyes.

Jasper kisses down my torso, sliding my pants off as he trails down my body. His kiss lands directly between my thighs. He absolutely devours me. He moans against my most intimate area, enjoying the pleasure he's bringing me. Within minutes, he has me crying out with my first orgasm.

"Fuck, little hellion. You're my favorite meal. I've missed your taste so much."

When did Jasper taste me? Was he pleasuring me in my sleep, and it wasn't just my delusions? I'm too drunk on lust to care about his admission at the moment. Realizing his slip up, he peppers me with kisses, making his way up my body. Jasper places a tender kiss on my lips. I can taste my sweet musk on them. Doing my best to pull his sweats off, his cock springs free.

While Tatum understood my father's rule of me not having sex until after marriage, he had me give him plenty of hand jobs and oral. If I was lucky, he rubbed my clit for a few seconds. He sure as hell never went down on me like Jasper just did.

Shit, I think Jasper got off on it as much as I did. Desperate to return the favor, my fingers run along his shaft. Shudders wrack his body as my grip makes its way up his shaft toward his head. Warm metal meets my fingertips. Instinctively, I yank my hand away.

Jasper chuckles, snatching me so we plop down on the small bed. With me straddling his thighs, he flashes me the underside of his cock. On the ridge at the base of his head is a vertical piercing.

"It's a king's crown, or a dydoe piercing, if you like it, I'll let you pick my next one," he says with a wink.

Acting on instinct, I move back far enough to lean down and flick my tongue over the piercing.

With a strangled groan, Jasper shoots up. His eyes are blown as wide as his pupils as he stares at me bewildered.

"Holy hell, give a man a warning next time. I'm on the verge of exploding, and there's only one place I want to come. I want you. Now," he growls. By the hungry look he's giving me, I, in fact, do not need to give him a warning next time and I'm welcome to do that anytime I'd like.

Shuffling back up his thighs, I straddle his cock. I slide myself along his shaft, and more importantly, his piercing. Both our breaths hitch at the sensation. Lifting myself up, Jasper guides his cock to my entrance while the other hand grips my hip.

Sudden nerves chill me. Goose bumps mar my skin as I allow him to guide me down. Once his head is past my entrance, I freeze. This doesn't hurt, it's fine. With both hands secure on my hips, Jasper takes over, thrusting in deeper. I'm so wet from my first orgasm, there's not much resistance and he slides half way in.

Hissing, I throw my face into the crook of his neck. This only pushes him farther inside me. The pressure is almost unbearable as our hips meet. I pray the pleasure will overcome the pain soon. Thankfully, Jasper silently gives me a moment to adjust.

With my eyes pinched closed, I try to kiss away the pain. He takes that cue to slowly guide my hips in a swooping motion, stimulating my clit on his pelvis.

Pleasure bleeds in, blanketing the initial pain. Needing to take control once more, I pull away from the kiss. I experimentally move my hips, finding what I like. Jasper's eyes instantly dart to where we are connected. Closing my eyes, I enjoy his sounds of pleasure. I hated hearing the sounds from the other men in the cells. But, hearing them come from Jasper has butterflies fluttering in my stomach.

A sharp inhale has my eyes flying open as Jasper's strong hands hold me in place halfway off his cock. His honey eyes can't decide if they want to settle on me or where we're connected.

"Are you on your period?" he questions, looking pained to have to ask right now.

Shaking my head, I see what has suddenly freaked him out. His cock is streaked with blood.

He throws his head back, pinching his eyes closed. Biting his lip, he gathers the courage to ask his next question.

"I'm your first, aren't I?"

I try to wiggle my hips so I'm seated fully on him, but he firmly holds me in place. As if remembering I can't use my voice, he peels his eyes open. I nod, giving him a soft smile to assure him this was my choice.

"Shit! I hope I wasn't too rough. Let me take care of you."

Jasper flips us so he's hovering over me. Surprisingly, the head of his cock never left me. Slowly, he thrusts all the way in. He keeps a slow, steady pace, monitoring my face for any signs of discomfort. His thumb rubs tiny circles against my clit.

A pounding crescendo builds as an orgasm threatens to consume me.

"Fuck, yes. Come for me."

Jasper's lips muffle my cries as my orgasm pulsates around him. His own moans are muffled by the kiss as he pants against my lips. His cock twitches inside me as warmth floods my pussy. A sense of accomplishment fills me, knowing I brought this man to ruin.

I expect Jasper to pull out and distance himself now that we both came. He keeps his cock buried deep inside me, flipping us so I'm straddling him once more. Using one hand on my hip, he keeps us locked together. His other hand splays across my back, pressing our chests together.

Perspiration covers our bodies, but I don't care. Ignoring the urge to lick the sweat from his pecs, I rest my head against them instead. A gentle kiss to the top of my head is all it takes for me to fall asleep in his arms once more.

CHAPTER 14

JASPER

God dammit. My little hellion gifted me with her virginity. Nothing and no one have so much as made my dick twitch, let alone get hard, in years. I've only had one other obsession, and it was at the height of my sexual curiosity in my early adolescence. I was morbidly curious about a fictional character. The first time I became aroused was for someone who didn't even exist. Self-gratification was as far as I got with that particular fantasy. Yet this vixen has had my dick rock hard since the day she was delivered to me.

For a while, I questioned if I was asexual or if my dick was just broken. I spent a lot of time at strip clubs, sex clubs, and paid for the best sex workers money could buy, from men and women alike. No amount of grinding bodies or porn has ever planted the faintest seed of desire.

I've never been particularly caring or attentive. So, the unfamiliar urge to take care of her and do everything in my power to make sure she's okay is new. Having someone in my personal space is also new. I've never cuddled until her, yet she makes it feel as natural as breathing.

I'm not sure what it is about her that has stirred my cock to life. All I know is now that the beast is awake, it's insatiable. Obsession takes hold, demanding I fill her with my cum every chance I get until she's swollen with my child.

I fuck my little hellion to sleep. Wrapping my arms around her in a safe cocoon, I refuse to pull out of her sweet cunt. As if sensing my cum leaking out of her, it hardens, sealing it in. Peering down at the burner phone, I decide on letting her nap for an hour before starting with the phototherapy.

It's half past four in the afternoon, so the lamp will need to be turned up a few notches. My little hellion swats me away when I try rousing her from her slumber. Once awake, she wordlessly demands chocolate and that I talk to her while she absorbs the UV rays.

Not wanting to lock her away in this bunker longer than necessary, I increased the intensity of the UV lamp a few extra notches. She's had enough time stolen from her, and I refuse to be another one of her captors. What she doesn't know is that she's never getting rid of me. Once we're out of here, she can live freely; just with me at her side.

Without the setting sun to lead our daily schedule, I have alarms set for waking us in the morning, meals, and a reasonable hour for bed. I chat with her about random nonsense as we sit in front of the lamp to help pass the time. I try getting a better understanding of why she's mute. It seems like she wants to talk but is unable to put sound to her words. She assures me I didn't miss some attack on her that would have damaged her vocal cords.

We sit together until the dinner alarm goes off. Trailing behind me, we peruse our canned options. She points out what she wants. Canned corn and ravioli is simple, but she beams at being able to make this small decision for herself.

"You did so well today. You did amazing tolerating the light, not complaining one bit. You're so strong, and I'm proud of you," I praise her as I massage lotion into her pink tinged skin.

Tears pool in her eyes and her lashes flutter rapidly, trying to blink them away. Taking her small hand in mine, I guide her to her bed to tuck her in. Kissing her temple, I whisper, "Goodnight," before slipping into my own bed. My message is clear; she doesn't owe me anything since she slept with me. Little does she know the gravity of what that moment means to me. She was my first, and I plan on her being my only.

A small body gluing itself to my back wakes me from my restless sleep. I bite back a chuckle, unwilling to let her know her presence awoke me. She's spooning me, tucking her icy hands under my shirt, splaying them across my abdomen. My little hellion is five foot nothing. She's like a little backpack trying to spoon my six-four body.

As if sensing I'm awake, she begins tracing letters on my back. With all the lamps off, there's no way for me to be able to read her lips. She traces two words; *safe, warm.*

Her breath hitches as I turn, pulling her into my chest. She practically crawls on top of me, turning me into her own personal bed. I don't object, her weight pressing against me is soothing.

I hold her to me like the precious gift she is. Slipping a hand under her shirt, I lazily stroke my fingertips along her spine in a whisper of a touch. With my other hand, I alternate massaging her scalp and stroking her hair. I make a mental note to tackle her tangles sooner rather than later.

I worked out a good portion of the tangles in the tub before we escaped, but running through the woods diminished my progress. I fight back the drowsiness until her breathing evens out once more. My last conscious thought is how I could get used to falling asleep with her in my arms.

The soft whirring of the lock of the bunker door disengaging snaps me out of my sleep. Rays of light flood the bunker. My little hellion hisses into my chest, still not used to the amount of sunlight flooding in. Men drop into the bunker, not bothering to be stealthy. Unwilling to focus on what they are saying, I focus on protecting what's mine. I flip us so I'm shielding her body with mine as I search the lining of the mattress for the compartment I have my knife and gun hidden in.

Cocking my head, I take in at least nine men in tactical gear invading our safe haven with weapons drawn. Their words filter in. They're asking for an Esmarie. Looking down into my little hellions wide, pain filled eyes, I know without a doubt they're here for her.

Don't get me wrong, I'm glad she has people who came for her, but that doesn't excuse the fact that they have guns pointed in the same direction as her. For all I know, these could be Ago Avanzo's men here to collect his latest doll.

They sound more pleading than threatening. Plus, they used her name, not little doll. I don't know who sent them, but I do know they aren't Ago or Sylvester's men. I swear to god though, if these idiots blow our cover and lead Sylvester's men straight to us, I'll give my life to kill them all before they can get their hands on her again.

Peering into my little hellion's hazel eyes, her confusion is etched into every one of her features. She doesn't recognize them either, nor does she know why they'd be looking for her.

"I'm going to lift my weight off you. I need you to crawl under the bed and go hide the best you can," I whisper, pointing with my eyes where I need her to tuck herself away to.

I see the trust in her eyes as she squirms out from under me. Clenching my jaw, I will my eager cock to calm down. The last thing I need is to face these guys with a fucking hard on.

"All right, enough with the guns. I'm going to slowly get off the bed. Don't. Fucking. Shoot," I command as I watch her pull herself to safety.

Holding up my hands in surrender. I face the intruders head on. Taking me in, they all tense, raising their guns once more. Geez, they act like they haven't seen tented sweats before. They need to fucking chill.

"Lower your gun, sir," one of them calls out.

Oh shit, I forgot that was in my hand. As a show of good faith, I move to place my gun on the ground when my little hellion darts out of her hiding place. Making a pained squeal, she places her body in front of mine. I'm well over a foot taller than her, so she's not shielding much. It wouldn't stop a head shot.

Her chest is heaving, and fuck knows how terrified she must be right now. I bite back my frustration that she didn't stay hidden when I realize she's trying to protect me. She must've realized that they're here to rescue her and wouldn't risk accidentally shooting her to take me out.

Panic sits thick in my throat at having so many guns aimed her way. Desperate to shield her body with mine once more, I scoop her up around her arms before spinning her away. Just as I'm turning, ringing ricochets through the air. A bullet rips into my shoulder. The searing pain is instantaneous, but I refuse to lessen my hold on my little hellion; on Esmarie. Such a beautiful name for a beautiful woman.

Esmarie covers her ears. My own are ringing, but I don't have to hear her to know she's crying. Through the ringing, I hear the distorted commands to not shoot. What fucking idiot fires a gun in a metal box?

I'm more worried that Esmarie got hit. I'm unsure if the bullet went through and hit her, or if it ricocheted and hit her. Needing to know she's okay, I place her on the ground. Frantically, I search her for any wounds. I could cry when the only blood I find on her is mine.

I don't have time to be angry at the men slowly approaching us from behind. My little hellion is having a panic attack. The only thing that matters is calming her down. She's frantically yanking at her clothes. I find my knife, ready to cut them off her to help, before remembering our company.

Cupping her face in my hands, I assure her we're all right with a forced smile. When that doesn't work, I pull her into my arms, hugging her tight. Swaying us gently, I keep murmuring soothing words.

I'm so focused on calming her, I miss her reaching around the ground, searching for something until it's too late. She stiffens in my arms, eyes locked behind me. With a trembling hand, she raises the gun. The shuffling behind us halt.

Before I can think better of it, I palm the hilt of my knife over the barrel of the gun. I'd rather take another bullet than risk any more bullets ricocheting at full velocity. This girl is determined to protect me, and that gives me a fuzzy feeling in my core.

Her eyes widen at what she's done. I refuse to flinch. Carefully, I reach up, empty the chamber, and flick the safety on. I leave the gun in her hand, letting it provide the sense of safety she needs. Bullets clatter to the floor behind us as our unwelcome guests do the same.

My little hellion lives up to her nickname once again. Deciding she's not done; she launches the now useless gun at the closest man. There's a grunt as it collides with its target.

"Okay. Now that that's out of the way, how about we all stay where we are and have a civil conversation?" a guy with dirty blonde hair says when I turn my head to determine if any of them are still a treat.

He runs his hand nervously through his slightly curly strands. He's the closest to us but appears to be the scrawniest. With no answers as to who they are or why they're here, I couldn't agree with him more.

CHAPTER 15

BECKETT

Esmarie is everything, yet nothing like I expected. Even with her bones protruding and a layer of grime clinging to her, she's still radiant. One thing is clear; Esmarie has gone through hell. Her fear wraps around her like a cloak. I try to minimize my presence by attempting to be the least bit intimidating as possible.

Fury courses through me as I take in her battered appearance, and I know I'm not the only one. One of her eyes is practically swollen shut, and bruises litter her face. The purple hue indicates they're recent. Inspecting the man's hands, there isn't so much as a lick of redness across his knuckles. It's unlikely he inflicted the blows, but his clear knuckles don't absolve him completely.

I'm not sure who this man is, or if he has connections to whoever Bruce sold her to. But whoever he is, he clearly isn't a threat to Esmarie. He's doing everything he can to keep her calm. She clings to him like he's her lifeline. Clenching my jaw, I hate that she's more scared of me than him. Regardless, we need some answers.

"Stay right where you are. Don't even try taking a single step toward her," the brooding man demands.

He rushes past us mumbling that we're going to get us all killed. With him being the bigger threat, we turn to face him as he passes by us. He makes quick work locking us all in the bunker. We're blanketed in darkness before he flicks on a lamp. He snags a first aid kit from the shelf before returning to Esmarie's side. I arch a brow, but say nothing as he slips a pair of sunglasses over her eyes.

Luckily, we brought Doc along. He makes quick work pulling out supplies to clean up the flesh wound Decker got with Esmarie's bullet projectile. Huffs, followed by deep rumblings to stay put draw my attention away from my men and back to my obsession.

She steps up to Doc with what must be her rendition of a scowl. In a fit of annoyance, she slaps his hand away from Decker, before making a feeble attempt to drag him over to the man sitting on the bed.

She hardly budges Doc an inch before she's panting heavily and sways as if she is going to faint. We share a look of concern before I nod to him to comply with her. Steadying her, Doc leads her back to the mysterious man.

The man looks feral before Esmarie drops Doc's arms and drags herself back to his side. His hand reaches for hers and instantly begins rubbing his thumb along the top of her hand. With one arm, he swiftly tugs off his shirt. With the ease he did it, you wouldn't expect that it was the side that just took a bullet.

"Let's get you patched up and take a look at your shoulder," Doc offers.

He lifts the sunglasses from her eyes, wiping away her tears. He's so gentle with her. I note how she doesn't flinch away from him. Giving a brief nod to Doc, he cranes his neck so he's staring into Esmarie's eyes. It's so intense, that if this were any other situation, I'd find it kind of hot.

Doc offers a quick apology before digging into his shoulder socket with forceps, searching for the bullet. Not once does he flinch.

One thing is still bugging me. Esmarie hasn't said a word this entire time. Why is she so silent? Breaking the silence, I state, "We need some answers."

"Agreed. Who are you and why are you here?" He doesn't so much ask but demands, refusing to look away from Esmarie.

Biting my tongue, I'm reluctant to answer his questions first. But, doing so may be the only way he'll work with us.

"We work for her family that cares deeply about Esmarie's wellbeing. We've been tasked with locating her and bringing her to safety," I offer enough of the truth to satisfy him.

Esmarie flinches, and he cuts us a sharp glare. So, she must know something about the people she knows as her family.

"Who are you, and why do you have Esmarie?" I quickly ask.

Ignoring us, he returns his attention back to her as Doc begins stitching his shoulder. Even without anesthetic, he shows no reaction. Is he a psychopath or a machine? I want to wince just watching. Just when I'm about to ask again, I catch a twitch of Esmarie's lips.

"Name's Jasper. I helped her escape. Her safety is all that matters to me."

"Okay Jasper, who did you help her escape from?" I try prying further.

"Sylvester runs a sex trafficking ring," he grits out, causing Esmarie to tremble. "We're here hiding from his men who are likely searching for us. I'll die before I let them get their hands on her again."

Scrutinizing him, I can't tell what his connection to the trafficking ring is. He obviously has some connection to know the name of the leader. I suspect he's refraining from saying more on Esmarie's behalf more than anything. I need to establish some trust if I'm going to get her out of this metal prison.

"We know how she got mixed up in it. I promise, we just want her safe. We have a private jet waiting to take her home, where she has an entire organization ready to back her. We did eliminate six assailants in our pursuit of finding this bunker. We have a team running surveillance, ready to provide cover once we exit." I look at Decker for confirmation before giving a temporary peace offering. "You can escort her with us if you'd like."

Finally prying his gaze away from Esmarie, he holds eye contact with each and every one of us. A sigh of relief escapes me when he offers one nod. With a command for us to grab the lamp, he slips sunglasses over Esmarie's eyes before grabbing a backpack and following us out of the bunker.

He's far too close to Esmarie as he helps her up the stairs. His chest is plastered to her back, preventing her from falling backward. One hand remains firmly on her hip, as if he's assisting in lifting her up the ladder. Once out, his arms band around her back and knees, scooping her up into his arms. She curls into him as he carries her the entire trek to where cars wait to take us to the awaiting jet.

***

On the jet, Jasper still refuses to let go of Esmarie. Luckily, he doesn't put up a fight when Doc tries hooking her up an IV. Surprising us all, he only inquires what fluids he's hooking her up to, then thanking him for his help.

Jasper sprawls across the lounge with Esmarie cradled between his thighs. She wraps herself around his good arm, latching onto him as if there is any chance he would leave her as she slept. I think he's the only thing bringing her enough comfort to sleep.

"Those bruises are recent, who did that to her?" I ask, desperate to know who needs to pay.

"While I was preparing our escape, the guards thought they could do as they pleased in my absence. I walked in on them holding her down while they were about to take turns with her. She was too weak to fight them off. They didn't need to beat her to restrain her. I would've killed them all, but getting her out was more important."

I silently stew at the news. I email the team of psychologists we have waiting, briefing them on everything we can to help determine her mental state. There's no doubt she's thoroughly traumatized. The question is, to what extent? We sit in easy silence until he breaks it.

"Some dickhead named Bruce was the one who brought her to us. What do you know about that?" he questions softly, being mindful not to wake Esmarie.

"Bruce was part of the security team we had following her. Esmarie was never aware of our presence; it's a big part of her life that's been hidden from her. He was working directly with Tatum and her sister Anastasia. William, the man who raised her, was behind setting her up to be married to Tatum when she turned twenty-six."

He nods along, taking in the information. Thankfully, he doesn't make me elaborate on why they were working against her.

"Are they dead? I took care of Bruce when she demanded to talk to my boss. She offered her compliance so long as he didn't get paid," he admits.

"So she was talking when she arrived? Is her silence a recent development?" My heart drops when he confirms my fears. Clearing my throat, I continue. "We took care of William. As for Tatum and Anastasia? I've been making their lives a living nightmare. I filed for an annulment on her behalf, although I may have overstepped."

A devious smirk crosses his lips. "Oh, I don't think she'll be mad about it. That was her second request. Keep making their lives hell." He chuckles.

Esmarie stirs, pausing our conversation. We sit in silence, eyes on her, until she settles once more. Stiffening, I remember the looming question.

"Care to explain why we found you with her? What's your connection to the sex traffickers?" I ask, masking the biting accusation.

Quietly, he recounts how his brother had debts with Sylvester. When he died, Sylvester dragged him in, demanding he take over working off his brother's debts. He never wanted this life, but he was stuck. He admits he was drawn to her immediately and was determined to do everything he could to keep her safe.

Jasper needed out just as much as Esmarie did. He helped her escape, faking their deaths. I send Liam a message asking him to sort out a new identity for Jasper.

"She looks so small and doll-like in your arms. How's she doing?" one of the operatives along with us asks causally as he passes by.

Jasper tenses. Jaw clenched, his eyes darken to black voids. If he wasn't so concerned about waking Esmarie, he would be vibrating with rage.

"Don't you dare call her that again. Wipe that fucking word from your vocabulary, got it? Make sure everyone gets the memo. No one is to use that word in any context or capacity around her. Otherwise, I will get stabby and carve out their tongues," Jasper threatens. His twitching eye makes him look completely feral.

As if sensing my unease, he runs his fingers through Esmarie's hair to compose himself. His eyes remain closed, focusing on the sleeping girl in his arms.

"She was supposed to be sold to a buyer; Ago Avanzo. He refers to the girls he buys as his dolls. The men had orders to allow him the honors to break her. Her time in captivity could've been much worse. That didn't mean they didn't taunt her with the nickname every chance they got. I don't even think she's aware of what that nickname signifies," Jasper informs me on a choked whisper.

Not holding anything back, he proceeds to tell me everything he's heard about Ago, and what he does to his "dolls". The details are so gruesome, I excuse myself as bile works its way up my throat. While I may not fully trust Jasper, I'll give him anything he needs for getting Esmarie out of their clutches.

CHAPTER 16

ESMARIE

My body is cradled in a pillowy cloud as the comforting aroma of santal and citrus wraps around me. I don't need to open my eyes to know Jasper is behind me, or that it's his erection pressing into my back. Neediness consumes me as I wiggle back into him. He groans softly into my hair, his strong hands flexing on my hip in an effort to keep me still.

Just as I think I'm making progress on moving his hand exactly where I want it, he murmurs, "We have company."

Hooded jade eyes blaze into me as if sensing my desperation. The glasses do nothing to hide his desire. I recognize him from the bunker. Unsure how to feel about his presence, all I can do is trust that he's safe if Jasper's allowing him to be in the room with us.

We have a silent stare down until I can no longer take the temptation prodding into my back. Reaching behind, I grab

Jasper's erection through his sweatpants. He lets out a hiss, finally letting me pry his hand from my hips. His fingers slip into me with ease, and he gladly takes over. Skilled fingers plunge into me as his thumb circles my clit.

I turn my head, wanting a kiss from Jasper. For once, his focus isn't on me. He doesn't look away from the voyeur in the corner as he graces me with a kiss. His message is clear; I'm his. His possessiveness only makes me want him more.

Jasper's fingers leave my aching pussy. Before I can object, he's turning my face back to the stranger. As soon as our gazes lock onto each other, Jasper's hand returns to the place I want it most. With renewed vigor, he keeps a maddening pace.

Both Jasper and I are panting as we put on a little show. The man's knuckles are white as he grips onto the armrests of the chair he's watching from. Considering the prominent bulge in his pants, it is taking everything he has to refrain from touching himself.

Jasper jerks behind me, wetness greeting my back as he takes me straight over the precipice of orgasm.

"That's my good girl. Feel better?" Jasper asks in a rough whisper.

All I can do is nod. Heat licks its way up my neck, settling in my cheeks. After living in a cell and being stripped bare for spray downs, having a one-man audience should be nothing.

"Hi, I-I'm Becket. Um, the jet has a sh-shower if you want to get cleaned up. You can borrow some of m-my clothes, and

Decker may have something that'll fit you," he offers, nodding to Jasper behind me.

Ice water may as well have been poured over me. A cold sweat breaks out across my body. Already knowing my fears, Jasper asks if a bath would be possible. Beckett shakes his head, brows furrowed at my distress.

Jasper pulls me into a sitting position facing him. Cradling my face in warm hands, he asks, "What do you need?"

Can't do it alone. Please, I ask, my lips moving while no words escape.

A kiss on my forehead has me melting into Jasper's arms. No matter what, I trust this man. He's kept me safe, and continues doing so.

"Here's the deal, Beckett. She's going to need someone in the shower with her. Preferably standing at her back, supporting her. I would do it, but my shoulder is busted and I need to keep the stitches dry."

I don't miss how he avoids mentioning the injury his hand sustained because of me. A courteous nod is all we get before he's striding out the door. My breath hitches as Jasper lifts me from the warmth of the bed.

Setting me on the counter, Jasper instructs Beckett to comb out my hair. Entranced, I watch as he makes quick work washing himself with the handheld shower head. He does his best to avoid his bandages as a comb fights its way through my tangles.

Beckett must have sisters. His efforts of taming the matted mess on my head is painless. Patiently, he works on loosening the tangles the best he can. His strategy of starting at my ends and working his way up the strands is more successful than I anticipated. He could've shaved my hair off and I wouldn't notice, my attention glued on the water running along Jasper's abs and off his cock.

The show comes to an end when he wraps a pristine white towel around his waist. In a few confident strides, he takes Beckett's place in front of me. A first aid kit is placed next to us, so he can take care of cleaning and rebandaging himself.

Becket removes his clothes, leaving on his boxers. Relief floods me at the respectful gesture. Jasper carefully undresses me, studying my face for any indication of discomfort.

My feet are on autopilot as I'm guided to the shower. My whole body locks up the moment the warm water cascades down my back. Reaching back, I lock onto Beckett's wrist. In my head I chant *I'm not alone. I'm not back there. I'm safe.* Beckett steps in closer, turning up the water temperature.

He gives me a minute to compose myself, before talking me through each step of the shower before he does it. The warning helps settle my nerves. No action or touch is a surprise, allowing me time to prepare myself.

Gentle fingers lather shampoo into my hair. His voice is soothing, and his gentle touch is making me sleepy. I sway on my feet before leaning back into him. Beckett is trembling as much as I am, and I can't figure out why. Is he nervous about this, or am I making him uncomfortable? Jasper comes over to us, taking over rinsing the suds from my hair as Beckett uses both hands to hold me upright.

Something familiar yet foreign pokes my back for the second time today. Beckett coughs, murmuring his apologies while promising me it'll go away if I ignore it. Jasper's face lights up with amusement. As confused as I am, a tiny part of me doesn't want to ignore it.

Together, they work a generous amount of conditioner into my hair. With some pointers from Beckett, Jasper takes on taming my hair alongside him. Wide tooth combs give way through the cemented strands softened by the conditioner.

Jasper leaves me alone in Beckett's care momentarily before returning with a crate. He places a towel to cushion the hard plastic, allowing me a place to sit in the shower. Beckett gives me the detachable showerhead so I can use the water to stay warm. Miraculously, the water is still steaming the room. For hours, these men alternate rinsing, conditioning, and combing my hair.

The thought of actually having to shave off my hair has tears running down my cheeks in tandem with the water spray directed at my chest to warm me. I'm not vain, but I don't want to lose another piece of myself. My head bounces between wanting my familiar wavy locks and chopping off anything linking me to the hell I endured. The rat's nest and my protruding bones are the biggest reminder.

Whoops of celebration echo within the shower walls as Beckett runs the comb freely though my hair. Not wanting to be shown up, Jasper doubles his efforts. I welcome the slight tugging against my scalp, so long as it's hurdling us toward progress. With one final comb through all over my head, lukewarm water washes away the last remnants of grime.

Fluffy towels are wrapped around me, bringing warmth back to my limbs. Jasper scrunches my hair in a hand towel, absorbing excess water as Beckett steps out. He returns minutes later with clothes for each of us. Haphazardly, they dress themselves before gently helping me into Beckett's sweatpants and hoodie. I bury my nose into the soft fabric, inhaling the subtle notes of iris and sandalwood.

Never in my life has a shower drained me to the point of exhaustion. Strong hands lingering on my lower back guide me back to the bedroom I woke up in. Where Jasper's hand is possessive, Beckett's seems to linger.

I cringe at the new bedding, not wanting to think about how dirty I was when we climbed in. A tray of fruits, cheese, and buttery croissants are waiting for us on a pristinely made bed.

"Eat something, then you can rest," Beckett murmurs, offering me a strawberry.

Curious as to how far I can push him, I make no move to take the strawberry from his fingers. Instead, I stare into his jade eyes, mouth open in challenge.

Cocking a brow, he slides the juicy fruit past my parted lips. Jasper watches in amusement, already propped up in the bed. Forgetting the strawberry, I join Jasper. He welcomes me with open arms. Beckett follows close behind taking a seat atop the covers next to me. He continues to feed me a croissant and bites of cheese while I snuggle into Jasper.

Full and warm, I fall asleep once more in the safety of Jasper's arms. Only this time, I reach out for hands that feel foreign in mine. With both of them watching out for me, I feel like maybe everything will be okay.

CHAPTER 17

ESMARIE

Outside the little bubble of privacy in the bedroom, a crowd of men are relaxing. Exiting, they all jump to their feet, with broad grins. Their excitement is contagious, but why are they all so eager to meet me?

Keeping a respectful distance, they each take turns introducing themselves. Frozen in place, I have no words, even if I could get them past my lips. Overloaded with the new information, I try to memorize names to faces; knowing it's going to be impossible.

Lastly, a mountain of a man greets me with a warm smile. He introduces himself as Decker, but I recognize him from the bunker. Mortification floods me. I tried to shoot him and was successful in grazing him with a bullet.

Chest tightening, my breathing quickens. What if he's mad at me, and the nice smile is just to trick me into letting my guard down? Instinctually, I take a step back, bumping into a solid wall. I allow Jasper's presence at my back to ground me. A hand grasps mine, offering a few squeezed in quick succession. Beckett's silent assurance has me facing the looming threat in front of me once more.

I try to offer my apologies, but my lips wordlessly ramble. Decker cocks his head to the side considering me in silence before glancing at the men behind me. I release a huff of relief when Decker strides away. The reprieve doesn't last long before he returns with a tablet in hand. Offering it to me, I take it with trembling hands.

Already pulled up is a blank word document. Quickly, I type out how sorry I am for shooting him. Unwilling to extend my arm, giving him the opportunity to grab me, I toss the tablet back to him.

Decker catches it with ease before reading my message. He releases a booming laugh, causing me to flinch and Jasper to tense behind me.

"It's all right, kiddo. You saw me as the biggest target and threat. You did the right thing aiming for me. It's just a little scrape. I'm already as good as new. Maybe when we get back, I can teach you how to shoot?" Decker's jovial tone has me relaxing.

I look up at Jasper behind me, searching for permission. I have no clue if that would be a good idea or not. A broad smile greets me as he nods his encouragement. Turning back to

Decker, I quickly nod. With a smile, he hands the tablet back to me before taking his seat once more.

Nestled between Beckett and Jasper, I listen as they chat. They have an easy camaraderie. Typing on the tablet, I ask where we're going. Part of me longs for the familiarity of my apartment, but I dread the possibility of seeing my husband and sister. All I want to do is cry in Brielle's arms while we eat our weight in ice cream.

Beckett frowns at me using the tablet to communicate with them before quickly replacing it with a smile. Jasper looks to Beckett, awaiting an answer.

"We're going to New York. That's where our headquarters is. Our boss, Mr. Beaumont, would like to meet you. Is that okay?" Beckett asks, nervously running his fingers through his wavy dark blonde locks.

I don't have my passport, and what about my friends and family? How will I get back? I try to object.

"It'll be fine. I have a new identity waiting for Jasper, and I've already ordered you new documents." Beckett is quiet for a while, avoiding my gaze. "I um... Well, I filed for an annulment on your behalf when we were looking for you. I'm sorry, I realize that was way out of line, but we have vetted and debriefed Ms. Carmichael. She is at headquarters, waiting for you," he admits.

Holy shit. Although I agree that it was a little presumptuous of him, it's hard to be mad since that's what I wanted ever since Baldie tossed us on that train. I'm only mad I didn't get to file myself, or witness Tatum's reaction. My brain catches up to the rest of his statement. He found the one person I've been dying to see, and she's waiting for me!

I squeal, launching myself into Beckett's arms. Without thinking, I press my lips to his before wrapping my arms around his neck. He's frozen beneath me. I wait for arms to wrap around me, but they never come. Pulling away, he stares at me with a stunned expression on his face. I think I broke him.

I realize too late what I've done, and now I'm practically straddling him. Fuck, Jasper. Whipping around, I expect to find rage filled eyes. We've never talked about what we are, but it feels like we're together. My cheeks flame when he smirks at me, offering me a wink.

Slowly, I climb off Beckett's lap. I want to climb into Jasper's but think better of it.

"He knows Brielle is your best friend, and she's someone you can trust. We want you to be happy. You'll have your own debriefing of sorts, and it's best that you have someone familiar in your corner." Jasper's softly spoken words set me on edge.

You guys are leaving me there? I accuse when his eyes land on me so he can read each word formed on my lips.

"No, of course not. I'll be by your side until you tell me otherwise. Even then, I'm not sure I'd be able to let you go."

I melt at Jasper's admission, and hear Beckett mutter his agreement. While I'm ecstatic to have my best friend with me, I can't help but wonder if what I'm about to walk into is so bad that they deemed it necessary to track her down.

***

A platoon of blacked out Escalades are waiting for us when the jet lands. Whispers of Beckett's touch linger on my skin long after he escorts me off the private jet, helping me into the SUV. Compared to Jasper's domineering touch, Beckett's is hesitant, but just as comforting.

Beckett and Decker urge me to get some sleep on the drive to what they call headquarters, but I'm buzzing with excitement to be reunited with Brielle. Sleep is out of the question. Plus, I've done enough sleeping on the flight to New York.

I stare out the tinted windows, watching the chaotic traffic fly by around us. We pass through heavily populated blocks with skyscrapers, into a quieter part of town. Traffic becomes scarce as we enter a pocket of serenity tucked away from the bustling city.

A concrete fortress looms up a long drive. The driver stops in front of the security gate, scanning a badge. The dark iron rods slide open for us moments later. As we approach, the building comes into focus. The modern contemporary architecture is both breathtaking and intimidating.

There, waiting for us in the foyer, is Brielle, bouncing in place. Abandoning Jasper's hand, I take off toward her. We collide, her meeting me halfway. She guides me to the floor, hugging me tightly as my knees give out. My eyes sting for reasons other than the obnoxious fluorescent lights. Tears burst from my eyes like a dam breaking. Every emotion I've bottled up since my wedding day is purged from my system.

She holds me as I sob uncontrollably. I don't have the mind to be embarrassed by the audience, or that snot is leaking into her chocolate brown hair. She's crying just as hard. Everyone but Jasper and Beckett leave us to have our tear-filled reunion in peace.

Sniffling, she pulls away. Her soft brown eyes take me in, before flashing to the men standing at my back. Her lip trembles when she smiles down to me.

"I'm so glad to have you back," she says, squeezing me once more. "Can they help me get you to your room?"

Still unable to form words, I nod. Gentle hands help us from the ground. Brielle holds my hand as Jasper carries me. Beckett lingers behind with my sunglasses hooked to the front of his shirt.

In the room, Brielle glares at the men hoovering in the doorway. "Give us some time alone," she demands.

Beckett all but drags Jasper from the room telling him to leave us to catch up. With the promise that I'm safe with her, the door clicks shut. We listen to their retreating footsteps before Brielle pulls my hands into hers.

"Es, I love you so much. I know they found that man with you, and there's no missing the intense way he watches you. If this is some case of Stockholm Syndrome, I can keep him away. Just say the word." Brielle broaches the subject without hesitation.

I go to argue that's not the case, but all that comes out is garbled squeak. She holds up her index finger as she springs from the bed. Moments later, she reappears with a whiteboard in hand. They said they briefed her. If she knows I've been mute, then what else did they tell her?

Before I can panic, I turn my attention to writing out my defense. I admit that it may have started off that way, but he's protected me since the beginning. I make bullet points of all the kindness he's shown me; underlining that he saved me from that hell.

I wait as she reads what I wrote. When she looks back to me, I use the sleeve of Beckett's hoodie to frantically wipe away the words. Immediately, I frantically write once more. Warm tears leak down my cheeks as I admit that while I don't know the full story, he knew something. It scared him enough to have him risk everything to get out of there.

Hesitating, I jot down the hardest admission. I felt my time down there was ticking away and I was on the verge of giving up. I knew there was another auction coming up. It's the only time the beatings and rape stopped and the hunger pains dissipated. They didn't want their merchandise bruised or starved to the point they can't walk. I was the only one left in the cells for all the other auctions. Deep down, I knew I wasn't going to be so lucky this time.

Brielle cries reading my words. She hugs me while we cry together. She promises me I'm safe now. Once our tears have run dry, she looks at me with red rimmed eyes and a devious smile.

"I think you have an ex-husband to haunt, and two men devoted to protecting you, giving in to your every whim."

Chuckling, I listen as she lays out her plan. She tells me how she convinced Liam to cyberstalk him. Tatum Carter is nothing but a man of habit, so it was easy to figure out where he'll be and when. He thinks I'm six feet under, but I'm about to be his worst nightmare.

There's no love left for Tatum, only a hunger for vengeance. Anastasia thought she could take my place in his life. It seems she found it wasn't as glorious as I made it appear. I'd say they deserve each other, but that would be too generous.

I overheard Beckett telling Jasper that William is dead while I pretended to be asleep. Brielle's plan is devious. Tatum will think he's being haunted by his dead wife, while Ana will be paranoid that whoever took her father made her their next target.

The last order of business for the night is cutting away the remnants of the biggest reminder of all I've endured. In the Jack and Jill bathroom connecting our rooms, Brielle chops off my hair. My dark auburn hair now lays just above my shoulders, accentuating my sharp jawline and protruding collar bones. I refuse to see myself as weak.

Looking at my best friend, it's not different enough. As if reading my mind, she expertly gives me curtain bangs. I've never had bangs before, but they feel fitting. I stare at my reflection, at the new woman looking back at me. She's ready to reclaim her life.

CHAPTER 18

Beckett

It feels good to be back within the familiar walls at headquarters. While we have our own houses, my family and Mr. Beaumont's inner circle have private rooms within headquarters. Sometimes we need to be available 24/7, and it's faster and easier to take an elevator than to drive through New York traffic at any given hour.

I don't have any cameras in the room Esmarie is staying in, and I plan on rectifying that first thing in the morning. Settling for monitoring the security feeds outside her room, I know Jasper is just as on edge about her being out of his sight. With his room next to mine, I hear the rhythmic thudding of his pacing steps.

Ever since Jasper gave me the name of the man who was planning to make Esmarie his next victim, Liam and I have done some digging. For someone committing such heinous acts, you would think he would have some form of cybersecurity. It took me less than five minutes to hack into his server.

Granted, it took me twenty minutes to hack into INTERPOL's database to see what they had on him. While they are investigating him for tax fraud, they don't have much on him. Luckily, we have access to the best hackers, and Ago Avanzo is our only target at the moment.

Liam and I stay up all night gathering every piece of evidence we can dig up. With access to his calendar and correspondence, it's clear that Sylvester is trying to delay the auction, frantically searching for any excuse for why he can't hand over his promised doll.

Unsatisfied, I move to digging into Sylvester. While we took out most of his men who were directly responsible for taking Esmarie, his reach goes far. He has sent out pictures of Esmarie, demanding they find someone they can pass off as her. That simply won't do.

Calling in every hacker we have, we trace back every email address and number that received her picture. Additionally, we hack into all their accounts and wipe all traces of Esmarie's pictures. To them, it'll appear as if Sylvester issued his order and forgot to include her picture.

As the sun rises, I tip off the Feds and Ago about the secret auction Sylvester is holding. With the help of our inside man, we will also organize a rescue squad to evacuate the girls before they're sold off. Hopefully, Ago will show up at the auction to confront Sylvester, where the Federal agents can apprehend them both.

As I'm about to hop into the shower, there's pounding at my door. A disheveled Jasper stands before me with bags under his eyes. He pushes past me, tossing his backpack on my desk, making himself at home.

"I need you to get Brielle down here for me."

Sending a quick text to the guard stationed in front of their rooms, I ask them to escort her here. Their response is immediate.

"She's being escorted now. I'm going to hop in the shower quickly before she gets here."

I take the fastest shower of my life, dousing myself in the icy water. I toss on the standard cargo pants and fitted black tee that make up our everyday uniforms here. There is a knock on my door as I'm lacing my tactical boots. Jasper beats me to the door, yanking it open.

Her eyes narrow at Jasper, pushing her tongue into the side of her mouth to bite back whatever is on her mind. She rolls her eyes at him when he motions for her to come in. Reluctantly, she does so.

We watch him as he pulls something from his backpack. He sets what he retrieved down on my bed with such gentleness one would think he was handling a bomb. Curious, both Ms. Carmichael and I approach.

"Is that what I think it is?" She demands on a sharp inhale.

"She was delivered in it and wore it until the guards ripped it off her the day we escaped. I bribed one of the other captives to fix it the best she could. I know it was important to her because she trained her eyes on it every time someone yanked it off her body on wash days. It wasn't until Beckett called you Ms. Carmichael that I put two and two together. Your name's on the tag."

Jasper has been nothing but strong and confident since I met him. I don't know what to do with the vulnerable, shy man in front of me.

"I made it for her as a wedding gift, but to say her wedding was a disaster would be an understatement. She ended up getting married in it when her sister sabotaged her original dress," she whispers before looking at me as if she tasted something bitter. "Also, please call me Brielle."

"Noted. What exactly do you want her to do with it? I mean, don't you think it'll serve as a reminder of marrying Tatum, or of her time locked in that cell?" I can't help but ask.

"The dress is important to Esmarie because I made it, not because she got married in it. Honestly, this thing is beyond salvageable. There, it was a link to me. I'm not sure how long you plan on keeping us here, but I could make her a new gown with enough adjustments if you could get me fabrics and my equipment."

"Give Liam a list of everything you need, and we'll get it delivered by the end of the week," I promise.

Since we sent Liam back and the newer recruits to go pick up Brielle once we found the bunker, he's been flustered anytime we bring her up. I have no doubt he'll bend over backward to fulfill any request she throws his way.

With that out of the way, my radio goes off, informing me that Mr. Beaumont is ready to meet with Esmarie. Jasper all but bounces out of my room, ready to see her again. I can't say I blame him, given that I feel the same way. Brielle and I follow him.

"Do I need to be worried about him? Like, is she safe with him? I know Es doesn't think it's a case of Stockholm syndrome, but is it right?"

"As much as I hate to admit it, she is probably safest with him. He already took a bullet for her, and his only concern was making sure she was okay. He would die before he let anything happen to her," I admit with a shrug.

She seems to consider my words. "I've seen the way you look at her. It's the same way he looks at her. So if you say she's safe with him, then I trust you."

There's no hiding the blush that creeps up my neck, staining my cheeks. If she can see how enthralled I am with Esmarie, it's only a matter of time before others notice. I need to be more subtle.

Stepping into Esmarie's room, we find Jasper twirling her hair around his finger. I stare at her in stunned silence, unprepared to see her with a new haircut and in a long sundress. Brielle offers her a protein bar with a wink before hooking arms with her and leading her out the door. Jasper flicks under my chin as he strides past me.

When we get to Mr. Beaumont's office, Decker's already there. Brielle takes a seat next to Esmarie in front of the large oak desk. Jasper sits on the sofa with his elbows resting on his knees. Decker and I assume a wide stance with our hands clasped in front of us on each side of the door.

Mr. Beaumont sits silently, taking in the sight of Esmarie before him. The tension in the air is palpable, and Brielle's having none of it. She whips around to face us.

"For fuck's sake, you're putting me on edge standing guard like that." Her eyes briefly flick to Esmarie, indicating she's clearly more on edge. "Take a seat next to Jasper, will ya?" she all but demands.

With a brief nod from Mr. Beaumont, we cross the room in two strides to take a seat by Jasper. Mr. Beaumont isn't an emotional man, but his eyes are watery as he smiles at Esmarie. He looks to Brielle as if asking if she can handle the news he's about to deliver. With a deep breath, he jumps right in.

"Esmarie, it is so good to see you again. I'm Emmett Beaumont, and I'm your dad. I thought I was keeping you safe by having my half-brother, William, raise you. I'm so sorry that I couldn't keep you safe."

Esmarie's sharp inhale is the only sound in the otherwise silent room. We hold our breath, awaiting her reaction. Mr.

Beaumont winces, realizing his delivery wasn't as tactful as he anticipated.

"William was behind pushing you to marry Mr. Carter, and subsequently the situation we extracted you from. I run BeauCrest, and we have access to the top professionals to get you all the care that you need," he continues.

"Why?" a cracked whisper cuts off his ramblings.

The hoarse voice came from Esmarie; her vocal cords strained after not being used for so long. We're so shocked that she forced the word out, Jasper and Brielle are sniffling. Jasper leaves us on the coach to kneel in front of her.

She quickly takes his hand, squeezing it until her knuckles are white. He gives her a big smile before rising and standing behind her, all without dropping her hand.

"W-why?" Esmarie tries again with the additional support at her back.

"Your mother was just as influential within BeauCrest as I am, and when she died, you were the sole beneficiary of her inheritance. She left you a trust worth $15.2 million that the lawyers were to inform you of, granting you access upon your twenty-sixth birthday. While we do have our fair share of enemies, it was William who was ultimately behind her death. We never suspected it was him until you went missing. That's why it was so important that he married you off to someone under his thumb."

By this point, Esmarie is quietly crying. Mr. Beaumont leaves his desk to kneel in front of his daughter. He offers her a tissue, which she gladly accepts.

"I'd like to get to know you, and have you stay here a while if that's okay with you?" he quietly queries.

Esmarie crashes into him, wrapping him in a hug. She cries harder into his chest as his enormous arms encase her. Tears fall from his eyes, disappearing into her hair.

"I'll set up initial checkups, and bi-weekly counseling sessions. Once you're cleared, we can start with those shooting lessons we talked about. Maybe Jasper and Beckett can work with you on self-defense if you'd be comfortable with that. Brielle can join, and I can train her so you're not alone," Decker offers.

I offer Esmarie a bottle of water before excusing myself. I won't have much time to set up the cameras, so I'll have to make it quick.

***

"Well, here you go. You're a new man Jasper Winslow. What's that saying? The best lie is one with partial truths?" I joke as I hand over his new identity.

With a shit eating grin, he pats me on the back before heading to Esmarie's room to escort her to her psychologist appointment like he's done the past few weeks. He went as far as insisting that he has his own counseling session once a week since he's there waiting for her anyways.

If I'm being honest with myself, a part of me expected him to bolt once I handed over the forged documents. Fortunately, I think my assumption was wrong, and he's not going anywhere. He helps Esmarie more than either of them realizes.

Every night since arriving at headquarters, Esmarie has screamed bloody murder through her night terrors. To no one's surprise, she instantly calms when Jasper wraps her in his arms. From that point forward, he's slept outside her door, waiting in case she needs him.

Eventually, he was told to join her if it was okay with her. She all but moved him into her room. Now, instead of watching the center of my universe in her bed alone, I watch as Jasper cuddles her throughout the night. Watching her is still my favorite part of my nightly routine, with or without him.

Fuck, if I'm not jealous of how she snuggles into him. I wish it were me stroking along her back with her leg hitched over mine. She would fit just as perfectly in my arms as she does his.

I suspect he's aware of the cameras I placed in Esmarie's room. He's been eyeing them the past few days. His suspicions came to a head during combat lesions. Esmarie is off watching her best friend train with Decker as Jasper and I get a drink of water.

"Do they know how much you like to watch her?"

"Wh-what?"

"I mean I'm assuming it's you watching through those cameras, otherwise I need to go on a little hunt." There's malice behind Jasper's threatening words.

Sure he's about to go on a warpath, I toss my head back on a groan.

"How'd you spot them?"

"Scoping out cameras is second nature. It's easy if you know what to look for. To say Sylvester was paranoid would be an understatement. As long as you're the only one watching, your secret is safe with me." Jasper winks before giving Brielle a break as he spars with Decker once more.

I swear he rivals Decker in hand-to-hand combat and easily out shoots him. At least I can feel at peace knowing he's more than capable of protecting her. With his skills, Sylvester should have made him an enforcer. He's been a valuable asset in renovating our security protocols and training measures.

Jasper notices everything pertaining to Esmarie. He catches every single one of my lingering touches. If she noticed, she hasn't acknowledged it. He, however, winks at me every time.

Just as I suspected, he never forgot all about the cameras in her room; he started teasing me. Standing directly in front of the camera, he blocks my view of Esmarie. He proceeds to stare into the camera as he strips, winking before climbing in bed with her.

Time is flying by, and while Esmarie is healing, she still isn't talking. I see the evidence of her healing as she grows bolder with touching Jasper. Already, I know tonight is different.

After Jasper's little striptease, she immediately begins kissing along his neck when he joins her. Her hands freely roam his body. I can't help but palm myself through my boxers, wishing it were me.

Jasper whispers something in her ear. He kisses her when she giggles. Desperate to hear that sound, I connect my headphones before unmuting the audio

I watch, entranced, as he pulls her oversized tee over her head. He pulls her back flush with his chest, exposing her perfect breasts. Jasper doesn't stop there, though. He shoves the duvet onto the floor. Hooking her legs outside his knees, he puts her pussy on display for me.

Every inch of her is perfect, and I'm a weak man when it comes to her. The minute his fingers plunge into her pussy, I pull my cock out. Stroking myself, I match the pace of Jasper's finger fucking her.

She hooks one arm back around his neck, increasing their connection. Whispering in her ear once more, she nods frantically. I pant just as heavily as she is, basking in the sounds her wet pussy is making. I come all over myself as Esmarie moans out my name as Jasper brings her to orgasm.

Fuck, I need to hear that again. So blinded by pleasure, I can't even question his motives. Quickly, I download that video to my server so I can replay her moaning my name every night.

Emboldened, Esmarie isn't done. With her ass up to the camera, she dives for Jasper's cock. Her legs are spread enough that I can see her dripping pussy. After a few bobs of her head down his length, her fingers make their way to her entrance.

Of course, she would be so turned on sucking his cock that she couldn't help but touch herself. My dick twitches back to life at the sheer look of ecstasy on Jasper's face.

Pinching his eyes, closed, he can't help but toss his head back muttering curses. Just as quickly, his head snaps down, locking his eyes on her. I fuck my fist once more, imagining the fuck me eyes she must be giving him.

When Jasper is on the cusp of coming down her throat, she pulls off him. Fast as lightning, Esmarie is impaling herself on his length. Jasper's eyes bulge, hands flying to her hips. Clearly, he's just as surprised by her actions as I am. I have never been more jealous.

She rides him with reckless abandon, taking what she wants from him. Endless curses fall from his mouth as he helps guide her hips along his cock. He palms the back of her head in a possessive hold as he crashes his lips onto hers.

She screams out against his lips as he shudders beneath her. He slowly thrusts up into her, fucking her through their release as I find mine once again. Jasper lies back down, pulling her with him. Esmarie falls back asleep with his cock nestled in her cum filled pussy. Although I'd love to clean her up or offer her some form of aftercare, she look's perfectly content where she is.

CHAPTER 19

JASPER

I know I promised Beckett the cameras would be our little secret, but I couldn't help coming clean to my little hellion. My therapist has been drilling me about the importance of honesty in forming healthy relationships. It was a risk telling her, but how could I not with the way she was all over me?

It was one thing for Beckett to watch me finger her on the jet. She could see him watching us. Guilt almost dampened my erection, because someone had already stripped away so many choices from her. Luckily, she was more than eager to have an audience. She's played coy, but I know she's noticed Beckett's touch lingering.

My little hellion has been repressed for so long, she's insatiable. Her lips wrapped around my cock so intensely that I was surprised when she decided to remind me how her perfect pussy felt. It took everything in me not to come as soon as she sank down on me.

As much as I love fucking my little hellion, I fear her increased sex drive could be a delayed trauma response now that she's safe. I voiced my concerns, seeking guidance on how to check in and pull back, and that pleasantly surprised my therapist. The last thing I want is to hurt Esmarie further, or make her feel like I'm rejecting her.

The next night, when her hand slides past the waistband of my boxers, I can't help the small groan that escapes. My larger hand engulfs hers, halting her tantalizing touch.

Pulling her hand away from my hard cock, I gently kiss her palm. My chest tightens at the sadness glazing her eyes.

"You know we don't have to do this every night, right?"

"W-what do you mean? Are you saying you don't want me?" Tears well in her eyes as she tries to blink them away.

"It's pretty obvious I want you; I just don't want you to feel obligated to do anything. I'd be more than happy to simply cuddle you all night. You're the most important thing in my life, and I don't want to jeopardize that. My therapist agrees that the hyper sexualization could be a response to what happened. I worry about you."

My hellion studies me for a moment. Heat licks across my face, embarrassed I let it slip that I've been getting my own help. A huge grin lights up her face; she's so beautiful like this. I pull her closer, and she snuggles into me.

Warm breaths puff against my chest as she finds comfort in my arms. If she could crawl under my skin, she would. Since she can't, she settles on getting as much skin to skin contact as possible.

With mutual understanding, we fall into each other's arms, doing nothing more than making out before cuddling each other throughout the night. Every night my presence keeps her night terrors away, strokes my over inflated ego.

***

Beckett and I are practicing ASL while Esmarie is with her psychologist. Since her voice hasn't returned, Beckett thought it would be nice if we all learned it. Beckett's phone going off interrupts our lesson. He reads whatever message came through with a frown.

"We've been summoned. Our presence is required," Beckett says, pointing behind him to the door Esmarie walked through twenty minutes ago.

Beckett looks concerned, whereas I'm more confused. Even if we weren't waiting for her in this place's idea of a waiting room, we would drop everything to come at her beck and call. Raising my fist to knock, it meets empty air. Esmarie's psychologist pops her head out of the narrow crack before waving us inside.

My little hellion's eyes widen when she sees us. Before we can even take a seat, she's frantically typing away on a laptop perched on her lap. They have an augmentative and alternative communication (AAC) set up for her therapy appointments so she can easily communicate with her psychologist. With the final tap on the keyboard, a soft generated voice fills the room.

"I like you both, and I want what I have with Jasper with both of you. I hope I haven't been reading things wrong, but I don't want to choose and I don't want to hurt anyone." The blush on my little hellion's cheeks contradicts her wide eyes and pinched brows.

I can't take my eyes off her, yet I feel the weight of everyone's eyes on me. They are trying to gauge my reaction to her news, and I suspect that wasn't how she or her psychologist were planning to broach the subject.

A normal person's reaction would be anger, but I've never been normal. If it weren't for the distress emanating from my little hellion, I would drag out the suspense.

Kneeling in front of her, she reaches for me. I gladly take her offered hand, rubbing my thumb over her forehead to release the wrinkles

"No need to worry, I assure you I'm not mad. You deserve all the love in the world. Now, if it were someone other than Beckett, that would be a different story." I wink at her, causing her lips to twitch in the briefest smile.

I look at Beckett, daring him to say something. He absolutely has feelings for her. I'm just unsure if he's cool with me being included in that. Darkness creeps into my glare, worried he's about to say something to upset her.

"You've enthralled me for longer than I care to admit. Jasper's right; you deserve the world. I wouldn't dare push him out so I could have you."

I have to fight back the snorting retort begging to be set free. I suspect Beckett's been in love with Esmarie far before he found us in that bunker. That, however, is not my truth to tell, so I remain silent.

We spend the next three hours discussing relationship dynamics and how we can effectively communicate in moments of jealousy or conflict. If the meek doctor disapproves of our relationship with Esmarie, she doesn't show it. Her compliance only benefits us as she lays out the fundamentals to making this relationship work.

With a final warning to take things slow, we exit the office. Because I've been staking my claim on her, it's second nature to walk with my arm wrapped around Esmarie, cradling her tiny hand in mine. Hesitantly, Esmarie reaches for Beckett's hand.

He flinches, surprised by her touch. Her fisted hand retreats at the perceived rejection. Beckett catches her fist, uncurling her fingers until he can slip his in between hers. My little hellion walks stiffly, awaiting judgment from any passersby. A soft sway in her arms replaces the tension as she basks in the confidence Beckett and I sandwich her in.

Since we already missed most of the scheduled combat lessons, I tug my little hellion and her new boy toy back to the room they put me in before I all but moved into Esmarie's. Beckett arches a questioning brow, but follows along like the good boy he is.

"I think we could use some time alone. Her room is her safe place, and I don't want to encroach on that," I offer with a shrug as if it weren't obvious.

Soft squeezes of my hand bring my attention back down to Esmarie. She smiles up at me like I just gifted her the world at her feet. Making it to my room in no time, I reluctantly drop her hand to unlock the door.

As soon as her hand falls away from mine, Beckett pulls her in front of him. He clasps his arms in front of her in a protective hug as he rests his head atop hers. Her hands reach up to hook over his wrists, holding him just as tightly. I expect a flare of jealousy seeing the center of my obsession cradled so comfortably in another's embrace, but it never comes. More shockingly, peace settles within my heart.

CHAPTER 20

ESMARIE

Warmth cloaks me in its comforting embrace as I cuddle between the two men I'm starting a relationship with. My friendship with Brielle aside, all other relationships in my life have been carefully manipulated and strategically cultivated. Under the guise of my protection, William took on the role of playing my father. Even my relationship and betrothal to Tatum was an arrangement chosen for me.

The decision to start a relationship with Jasper and Beckett is solely mine, with their agreement. Terrible circumstances brought us together, but they've helped me heal every day without any titles or expectations.

Jasper's easy acceptance of this surprises me. Knowing him the longest, I naturally drift into his arms. Tender lips press to my forehead as he passes me into Beckett's welcoming arms. I'm pleasantly surprised by how easily the foreign arms transform into another safety net to hold all my broken pieces together.

Pounding on the door interrupts the moment of serenity. Jasper leaves me in Beckett's arms as he rushes to the door to stop the persistent knocking. He easily catches Brielle's raised fist that's still intent on knocking, before it can hit him in the face.

She shoves Jasper to the side, letting herself in with a dramatic exhale when she sees me. She doesn't react to seeing me in Beckett's embrace.

"Bitch! You missed combat training, then you weren't in your room. I was worried sick and had to enlist Liam to help track you down. It's time for dinner with Daddy Beaumont. Chop, chop. My worry worked up my appetite," Brielle chides as she drags me from bed.

Jasper's glare melts away at the sound of my giggle. Brielle and I have always used bitch as a term of endearment rather than an insult, something Jasper clearly doesn't understand. Thankful that Brielle's treating me the same as she always has, and not like the broken woman I've become, I try desperately to release the words waiting on the tip of my tongue.

Brielle and I walk with our arms linked as she squeals in my ear about what she just walked in on; promising to pry the juicy details from me later. My men follow close behind, leaving us to our girl time. My father's welcoming smile at the head of the table falters slightly as Brielle offers her seat next to me to Beckett with a conspiratorial wink.

Emmett's silent observation grates on my nerves. Under the table, both my hands reach out and hold onto their thighs in an effort to calm my raging panic. Simultaneously, their hands slip under my grasp entwining our fingers. My men must be on the same wavelength, because they plop our clasped hands on the tabletop.

My eyes frantically bounce between my pinned hands as if it's a scandalous secret they just exposed. Emmett remains silent, hiding any hint of judgment. Sweat beads on my forehead trying to find an explanation to give him. I just met him, what if he's disappointed he's finally reunited with his daughter, only for her to be a whore?

"Esmarie, are you okay, dear?" Emmett asks. His mask slips exposing his fatherly concern.

My mouth gapes like a fish out of water. Beckett's palm is slicked with perspiration, nervous about the reality of our situation.

"We're in a relationship with your daughter, sir." Jasper boldly states, not having any of the same reservations.

"Is this true, Esmarie?" My father asks.

I nod my head quickly, as my heart rate skyrockets.

"Pray tell, Beckett, how this relationship with my daughter developed? I can understand Jasper given he risked his life to save her. But you? You were supposed to be watching her. Do you think you can get away with taking advantage of her vulnerable state like this?"

I flinch at my father's ruthless tone. Clearly, he isn't happy with his employee going after his daughter. Anger builds in my chest at his implication that I'm something weak he took advantage of. This was my choice and not once did Beckett pressure me. He's been nothing but respectful. Hot tears prick my eyes as my frustration grows, wishing I could force out the words to defend him.

"With all due respect sir, you have the wrong impression. I understand I'm crossing a professional line, but I have nothing but your daughter's best interest in mind."

"So, what? Both of you are her boyfriends?"

"Yes." Jasper's confident response rings out, morphing into uncertainty. "That is, if that's what she wants." His honey brown eyes turn toward me, searching for an answer.

My nod of confirmation brings a dazzling smile to his lips. My father's chin rests on his propped hands as he comes to terms with the news.

"I can easily make both of you disappear if you hurt my daughter. I just got her back and I will not allow this new relationship to hinder her progress. Regardless, I've seen how dedicated you've been to her. If this is what my daughter wants, then you have my full blessing," Emmett reluctantly concedes.

The collective sigh of relief is palpable. In the next minute, servers bring in our entrees. My plate differs from those around me with my nutritionist's carefully curated meal plan. I sigh at my grilled chicken, trying to not eye Beckett's perfectly rare steak. Without a word, he slices a chunk off, offering me a bite. My eyes lock on his as my lips wrap around his fork, taking the tender slice of meat.

My father cuts the tension with an exasperated sigh. Returning my attention back to my plate, half of my chicken is gone. In its place is a chunk of juicy steak. It's no doubt Jasper's doing in my moment of distraction.

"So, Mr. Beaumont, can Esmarie and I borrow your private jet for the weekend? Esmarie's bodyguards can accompany us. No arguments from me," Brielle propositions.

"Please, just call me Emmett. That goes for you boys as well. Do I even want to know what you have planned?" He sighs.

"Well, Esmarie and I concocted this plan on her first night here. She's been making so much progress. Think of it as a reward!"

My father rubs his temples. "Get to the point, Brielle."

"Jeez, don't be a grump. Given the fact that Tatum the Twat thinks Esmarie is a ghost, it's only fair she haunts him." Brielle says with a shrug. "Trust me when I say, these two won't let her out of their reach. Decker can come too, if that makes you feel better. Liam can send you an entire itinerary of where we'll be, down to the minute." Brielle clasps her hands in front of her, pleading.

Jasper lets out a bark of laughter as a malicious smirk lifts my lips.

"Please," I manage to rasp out.

All heads whip my way. I greedily chug down water, soothing the strain the single word inflicted on my throat. I've spent the past month and a half healing and trying to get my voice back. I think some revenge is just what the doctor ordered.

"Damn, how can I say no after that? All right, but I expect constant updates. You better return my daughter to me safely."

***

On the jet, Brielle pulls out a large box. She's vibrating with excitement, waiting for me to open it. Jasper gives a knowing look, bracing a comforting hand on my knee. Luxurious merlot fabric is exposed as I pull the tissue paper away. Lifting it out, it's a close replica to the gown she designed for my wedding day. Only, this one has a higher slit and more intricate beading along the corset.

I stare in awe at the masterpiece. A confusing barrage of emotions chokes me. In captivity, my dress was my safety net. It was my only connection to the outside world and a reminder that at least one person would be looking for me. I withered away in that dress, but this one represents the woman I've changed into.

"Now, I can't take all the credit. Jasper brought me your dress. It was his idea to revive my gift to you, but having it differ enough to not be triggering."

Tears pool in my eyes, and for once, I make no effort to hold them back. I hug the dress as their arms wrap around me. I video call my father to show him my gift. Even through the screen, I can see his eyes misting over.

Brielle sits on the armrest, hugging me as the guys go over our plans for the morning. Decker, of course, is still griping that this is immature. His mischievous smirk contradicts his words, showing he's excited by the prospect of psychologically fucking with the remaining people who turned my life into a living nightmare.

A fleet of blacked out SUVs escorts us through the familiar streets of Montreal. I knew my father had money given the trust I have yet to touch, but the exclusive luxury hotel we pull up to is something out of movies.

Brielle is grasping onto my arm as if she is about to faint at the sheer luxury. Intricate chandeliers dripping in crystals glisten, and the marble floors are polished to the point we can see our reflections in them. Men in tailored suits offer flutes of bubbling champagne on golden platters as we wait for Decker to check us in.

Stern faced, Decker nods toward the elevator with two pearlescent envelopes in hand. With the swipe of one of the keycards, the elevator takes us to the top floor.

"Mr. Beaumont reserved both presidential suites for the week. Brielle, you and Esmarie can take one and we can share the other," Decker says diplomatically, as if reciting the instructions given to him.

"Oh, no, no, no. Es will share a room with her lover boys, and you and I can share. The couch is already calling your name," Brielle argues, gaining a disapproving scowl from Decker. "Plus, wouldn't she be safer with them there to protect her? I'm just a girl Deck. Anyone wanting to get to her would have no problem overpowering me." She huffs plucking an envelope from his hand, striding out of the elevator.

"Behave," Decker commands pointing between the two men flanking me.

As if it pains him, he hands the key over to Beckett before trailing after Brielle.

Two warm hands on my waist lead me into our room. The closet alone is larger than the entirety of my apartment. A private pool lays flush with the marble floor in front of floor to ceiling windows offering a breathtaking view of the city.

With a mischievous smile, I slip out of my clothes. Jasper catches on, and strips down. He beats me into the pool, uncaring of the water sloshing all over the pristine floor from his cannonball. A giggle escapes my lips as I jump in after him, right into his arms. Jasper wraps himself around me protectively at my back, peppering kisses along my neck.

Eagerly, I look to Beckett, imploring him to join us. The cutest pink flushes his face. Any reservations I had of being nude were forcefully stripped from me. I belatedly realize he hasn't been forced to become accustomed to it like Jasper and I. Being nude in front of Beckett is much more personal.

Before my excitement can falter, Beckett clears his throat before stripping away layers of clothing. I greedily take in his body. Defined muscles lurk under his seemingly scrawny frame. My eyes are drawn to his glorious cock. Jasper sputters dramatically, releasing me to clutch his chest.

"Where do you hide that monster of a cock Beck? Please tell me that damn thing doesn't grow anymore when it's hard. My ego can't handle it."

Unlike Jasper, Beckett carefully slides into the temperature controlled chlorinated water. Jasper presses a claiming kiss to my lips before launching me out of the water at an unsuspecting Beckett. Giddiness fills me, seeing such a playful side to Jasper. I land in a splash just shy of Beckett's arms.

I allow myself to sink to the bottom, remaining underwater until my lungs scream for air. Launching myself toward the surface, I wrap my limbs around Beckett in a sneak attack. He shakes his head at our nonsense, chuckling softly. The mood shifts when he kisses my nose. I stare at his lips before meeting his eyes, seeking permission.

Beckett takes the initiative as he presses his lips to mine. His kiss is gentler and exploratory compared to Jasper, who takes what he wants with his lips. I eagerly take everything Beckett offers, biting his lower lip, begging for more. His tongue slips in as our kiss deepens. Tension builds as the kiss remains slow and passionate.

There's no hiding how much I'm affecting him with our chests pressed together. His breathing is rapid as his hands grasp my waist, keeping me from grinding along his hardening cock. Beckett groans against my swollen lips as his body goes rigid against me.

"Fuck. Oh, fuck, I'm sorry," he pants softly, not meeting my eyes.

Jasper's dark chuckle echoes through the room. "Don't be ashamed, man. The same thing happened to me the first time I had her body pressed against me, and she didn't even kiss me."

What the hell are they talking about? I look between the two of them, waiting for someone to explain. My heart sinks as Beckett pulls me from his body, creating a distance between us. His face is deep scarlet as he stares at the white ribbons floating in the water.

Pride swells in my chest knowing I got him off with a kiss alone. Jasper steals me away, lifting me from the water until the cool marble meets my ass.

The room flips as I'm tossed over Japer's shoulder as he carries me to the oversized freestanding tub. Beckett quickly showers before trading off with Jasper combing my hair. Once they're both clean, they focus their attention on lathering my hair and body within the confines of the tub.

The tub is big enough to easily accommodate all of us. Maybe tomorrow I'll have enough courage to ask them to join me. Right now, I'm too excited to be cradled between my two boyfriends for the first time. After the explosion of chemistry with Beckett, my pussy is desperate to be filled.

Unable to help myself, I grind my ass against Jasper. His fingers tease my clit, frustrating me more. Thankfully, he takes mercy on me. He pulls Beckett's hand to my core, guiding his fingers in. He looks on the verge of losing control as his fingers pump into me. My arousal is evident by the squelching noises surrounding us. Jasper's fingers rubbing tight circles over my clit offer little relief as they bring me to orgasm. The hunger in their eyes is a dead giveaway that they plan to do this all night.

CHAPTER 21

JASPER

Before the first rays of dawn touch the sleeping world, Decker brings over a barely conscious Brielle. Beckett sets up the body cams to a live feed for them to watch from his laptop.

Our first matter of business is getting their fear and paranoia rolling. Anastasia is the easiest target for this. Not only does she know of her father's untimely end, since Beckett blocked all her funds, she's alone in that mansion. The dumb bitch still insists on going for a run at five in the morning without her security detail keeping watch.

What she doesn't know is that her running path just happened to need urgent repairs, so the concrete is torn up, ready for a team to pour fresh concrete. The princess is too vain to risk getting dirty running on the damp unpaved trails. Our job will be easy. She'll be uneasy running in a new location. If she catches us and has the balls to say something, we can easily explain away our presence as this being the route we run every morning.

My girl sends me off with a big kiss, much to Decker's chagrin. Brielle whistles and teases the grump by offering the same send off. In the elevator, Decker quietly stretches as I bounce around, excited for the chase. The valet has an SUV waiting for us.

Cloaked in the remnants of the night's shadows, Decker and I are lurking in wait. Our black joggers blend into the night, and our hoods pulled over our heads give us more anonymity. Beckett's voice trickles in through our earpieces. He's tracking Anastasia's location through her phone, giving us directions so we can intercept her.

Right on cue, a figure moves with determination. Decker and I hold back, lingering in the shadows until she passes us. Just as she goes to turn the corner, we give chase.

We jog easily, matching her pace. We get close enough to alert her of our presence, like a ghost lurking on the edge of one's reality. Our hunt is a delicate dance of creeping close enough to alert her of our presence, and ducking away out of sight as she turns around to survey her surroundings.

We continue our charade, weaving ourselves into her psyche. The threads linking her to sanity pull taut as we test the limit of her nerves. As we get closer to her, and delay our disappearance, we unsettle her even more. She knows she's being followed.

She's constantly looking over her shoulder, trying to catch more than a glimpse of us.

She thought she was safe in the early hours, when the world is quiet and peaceful. With a nod, Decker and I split up. He veers off our path to get in front of her. Impatient with her slow jog, I run up right behind her, finally confirming our presence.

I bump into her as I pass her, not turning to acknowledge her. Predictably, she starts hissing accusations of me following her. Her shrill voice dies off as I turn the corner, leaving her behind. Distracted, she doesn't notice Decker running toward her. I hope my hellion is getting a good view of Anastasia's terror through the hidden body cam.

As I jog back to the SUV, Decker's chilling voice comes through to my ear.

"You should be careful running all alone out here, Ana. You never know what monsters are lurking around the corner." It comes off more of a threat than a warning.

Minutes later, he's hopping behind the wheel to take us back to the hotel. We laugh together, and he admits he had more fun toying with the girl than he expected. There's a certain acceleration in inflicting psychological warfare on an unsuspecting but deserving individual.

Before I'm through the door, a tiny body collides with mine, entrapping me in its small limbs. I could get used to my little hellion greeting me like this. Not one to pass up the opportunity, I cup her ass as I carry her to the living room where the others are waiting. Brielle offers a slow clap.

"What in the actual fuck is that shit?" Decker asks, horrified.

I was too consumed with my girl to notice the creepy ass doll with an eerie resemblance to Anastasia.

"That's just a voodoo doll I made of the bitch. I even had one of your cronies sneak into her house and steal the hair from her hairbrush. Es gave great instructions to find her room," Brielle says with way too much enthusiasm.

"Hey, don't look at me like that. It wasn't just my idea. Es convinced Beckett to get cameras set up in their dining room so when the pretentious bitch goes to have her dinner, we can watch the moment she finds our gift," she says, glaring at us.

"They also want to fill the room with surveillance photos of her and her father. That doll will just be waiting on an altar as the table's centerpiece," Beckett divulges.

Decker is typing away, probably informing Emmett of the new development and having reinforcements sent in. Beckett gets to work on gathering photos of Anastasia and assures Decker they'll be ready for pickup within the hour. I suppose with enough money you can get hundreds of photos of stalked prey printed without questions or reports to the authorities.

Brielle seems all too pleased to have endless money to purchase everything for her demonic display, knowing Decker is about to be subjected to her madness. Reluctantly, I drop Esmarie into Beckett's lap so I can shower off the remnants of sweat clinging to my skin.

Steam fogs the glass panels. Cold hands snake up my torso, trembling against my reddened skin. My little hellion has a strong aversion to showers, so I'm surprised she's joined me. She props her chin on my sternum, smiling up at me, attempting to mask her fear.

Her breasts rub against my abdominals as she presses up on her tiptoes, reaching for a kiss. I happily oblige, and the kiss quickly morphs into something more carnal. My little hellion pulls away all too quickly. She trails kisses down my body until she's on her knees. My cock jumps at the sight.

I lean over her, bracing a hand on the glass behind her, blocking her from the shower spray. Beautiful hazel eyes lock on mine as she takes my cock in her mouth. My eyes roll to the back of my head as she gags slightly. God damn.

Her hand massages my balls as she sucks my cock with so much enthusiasm, I'm about to explode down her throat.

"Fuck, you're doing so good. I'm so close. Let me fuck you, please. Please hellion, let me fuck your tight pussy till I fill it with my cum," I beg.

My legs quake with the effort of holding back my orgasm. I'm seconds from having to physically pull my cock out of her mouth when she pulls off with a loud pop. My knees buckle slightly before I can catch myself.

Before I can regain my composure, my little hellion is climbing me like a goddamn tree. Hooking my arms under her knees, lifting her enough for our lips to crash together once more. Without guidance, my cock sinks into her tight pussy. Our moans vibrate against each other's lips.

Esmarie tries desperately to roll her hips against me, needing more than the shallow thrusts I'm giving her. Pinpricks of pain dance along my scalp with how hard she's grabbing my hair. I pull away enough to be able to read her lips.

"What do you need, little hellion?"

Your cock. Fuck me like you mean it Jasper, she mouths.

What my little hellion wants, she gets. With a hand cushioning her head, I pin her against the glass. She jumps when her warm skin meets the chilled glass.

"I'm not going to last long, I promise to take care of you after."

Her eyes twinkle with mischievous glee. She knows the effect she has on me. I snap my hips roughly, uncaring of the matching bruises we'll be sporting tomorrow. Her nails dig into my back, demanding more. One at a time, I pull her legs until they're resting on my shoulders. She cries out as my cock pounds deeper.

I've held back for as long as I can, but her moans of pleasure send me over the edge. Strings of expletives fall from my lips as I praise her. My words affect her. Her pussy grips my throbbing cock.

Fumbling to shut off the water, I make quick work of drying us off so we aren't soaking wet. With my cock still buried in her, I sprint to the room. Beckett jumps, surprised by our sudden appearance. Before he can get a word in, I'm already diving between my hellions' legs.

Uncaring that my cum is dripping out of her swollen pussy, I devour her. I could have done this in the shower and spared the bed, but I wanted to tempt Beckett. I know my little hellion wants him, but neither is willing to make the first move. Unfortunately, I'm too determined to have my hellion squirting on my tongue to tell him to join.

My little hellion is nothing but demanding when it comes to her pleasure. Her hand reaches out, slapping the bed next to her in a silent demand for Beckett to come closer. He slides in next to her, and she lets out a feral growl when hands meet pants instead of his bare cock. She claws at him, desperately trying to pull his pants off.

Beckett awkwardly fumbles, pulling off his pants. I swear the man's a virgin. Esmarie's pussy constricts around my fingers as soon as her hand wraps around his cock. She effortlessly pumps his cock, twisting slightly around his head before stroking back down his cock.

I'm nothing, if not devious. Taking a page out of Esmarie's playbook, I wait until she's on the verge of orgasm. In one fluid movement, I'm lifting her from the bed. My hand replaces hers on Beckett's cock as I guide her down along his length.

Full body shudders consume Beckett as my little hellion cries out. His knuckles are white on her hips. Even though I warmed her up, she's going to need a moment to adjust to his size. I try not to think about how big he felt in my hand in the brief moment I guided him in.

With jerky movements, Esmarie tries riding his cock while on the edge. Beckett is too dumbstruck to do anything but hold on to her like his life depends on it. I put pressure on the back of her head, moving her closer to Beckett. He meets her halfway, claiming her lips.

Ignoring my now throbbing cock, I take over. Mimicking the motion she uses when she rides me, I guide her along Beckett's shaft. It only takes seconds before she's trembling, crying out her orgasm.

"Ah fuck. Oh Fuck. Fuck. Fuck Fuckkkkk," Beckett cries out as Esmarie milks his cock.

Even though this was my doing, I can't help the sparks of jealousy. My cum should be filling her. Considering he's still shuddering beneath her; he's still pumping cum into *my* pussy. It's illogical to think his cum is replacing mine, but I wish I didn't clean my cum from her pussy with my tongue.

Needing to rectify the situation to sate my jealousy, I lift her until his cock slips free. Unwilling to wait another second, I plunge my cock into her pussy. If Beckett minds me fucking Esmarie on his lap, he doesn't object.

Reaching around, I have no mercy rubbing her clit. The taste of her orgasm on my lips revived my cock, and watching her pussy stretch around his cock put me on edge. It's a race to our orgasms. I kiss along her spine as she kisses Beckett. The slight movement of her shoulder is the first giveaway that she's pumping his cock once more. The second is the moans falling from his lips.

Not one to be outdone, I don't hold back my own moans of pleasure. My hellion's pussy loves it when we're vocal. Pleasure zaps up my spine until I'm filling my girl once more. Her pussy contracts around me until the pressure is too much, and she explodes, drenching us in a tsunami of her pleasure. Beckett curses out his release, marking Esmarie's perfect tits with his cum. It's a beautiful sight; one I could get used to.

CHAPTER 22

Esmarie

Mercifully, we didn't have to wake up before dawn for today's itinerary. That didn't stop Jasper from leaving me in bed with Beckett to go swim laps. I sip my raspberry matcha, too nervous to eat the brunch my men had no problem ordering. I force myself to eat some berries to appease them.

Beckett's phone vibrates with a video call from my father as fists pound on the door. Beckett greets my father as Jasper stalks toward the door.

"Good morning, my dear. I have a surprise for you."

As if on cue, voices fill the suite. Brielle bounces over with a few women trailing behind her. They make quick work unloading the train cases they rolled in behind them. Decker hands me a small velvet box with a soft smile. Jasper shoots daggers at him as I pluck it from his outstretched hand. I stare at the ring, confused, when my father's voice cuts in.

"That was your mother's ring. I had it resized in hopes it'll bring you strength. Brielle redesigning your dress made me think you should resemble his last memory of you. I hope it's not too much, but the girls are available to do your hair and makeup for as many days as you want to torture that man." My father's voice cracks with emotion as he watches me slide the ring onto my finger.

The weight of my mother's ring is comforting compared to the gaudy diamond Tatum bought me. Suddenly choked up on emotions I nod my acceptance of his plans, offering him a watery smile.

My father chats idly with Decker and my men while the women make quick work of my hair and makeup. Brielle beams next to me. Once finished, Brielle pulls me into the master room to help me into the gown. I stare at myself in awe as she tightens the laces to the corset.

My hair and makeup didn't look this good on my wedding day, and it's a testament to everything that went wrong that day. Everything about that day was planned with little consideration and cheaply hired. These women are welcoming and make me feel beautiful. There're no snide looks or barbs thrown my way to cut me down. It's the experience I wish I had that awful day.

All conversation stops as Brielle parades me back to the others. The women look at me, prideful of their exceptional work. Decker looks just about as emotional as my father. My men look absolutely ravenous for me.

The women offer me a quick hug before they excuse themselves. I'm taken aback by their kindness. My father assures Decker that he has a secondary team watching William's estate. Once Anastasia leaves, they'll install cameras and set up the "room of horrors" as Brielle insists on calling it.

Now, more than ever, I wish I could tell my father how thankful I am for everything he's done for me. With all the determination I can muster, I clench my best friend's hand.

"Thank you, Dad," I say out loud, my voice raspy from disuse.

"You're welcome, my dear. Have fun today and give them hell," my father says on a choked sob.

My feet leave the ground as Jasper spins me in circles. His pride and excitement are palpable. I wish I could get myself to say more to everyone here with me. They make me feel safe; like I have a home, where I belong.

***

Jasper advises that my haunting of Tatum needs to start inconspicuously. Just like Ana, I'll linger long enough for him to get the briefest glance of me from the crowded street. We'll play on the innocuous moments where he can feel our eyes on him, but he'll never quite find me until I'm ready.

We follow him throughout the day. I get a lot of curious glances walking the street all done up. If we were in New York, no one would bat an eye. Beckett used some voice memos I'd sent to Brielle to create new recordings. Extra foot soldiers who specialize in blending in with crowds follow Tatum, playing the recording of my voice delivering taunts.

Hearing my voice was the insidious seed planted into his mind that blossomed into his undoing. Within the hour, he was skittish, searching for where my voice was coming from to no avail. By dinner, his paranoia was apparent to onlookers.

Tatum made a frantic phone call, and twenty minutes later, my dear sister pulls up. There's a familiar closeness between the two I've never noticed before. Whether it's a recent development, or something that's been there all along makes no difference to me. Brielle and I share mischievous smirks, knowing the team is setting up Ana's next surprise.

For hours, I toy with Tatum, letting him catch the briefest glace of me. I have far too much fun lurking in the shadows, being nothing more than a phantom of a familiar silhouette hunting him. Slowly, his confusion morphs into denial. After all, it couldn't be his dear wife; he sent her off to her death.

I want to seep into his thoughts like poison. In the crowded street across from where our targets sit for dinner, I stand tall. Vulnerability creeps in, not having my men directly at my back. They're close enough that I know I'm safe and they can hide me away in a moment's notice.

I let my stare bore into the traitors as I stand there like a ghost who is always lurking nearby. Little by little, we've chipped away at their sanity. Their exposed nerves unwoven and exposed by our hands. I fight the urge to fidget, as I continue to go unnoticed.

A beam of light flashes across their faces, drawing their attention toward me like a beacon. Brielle laughs maniacally, crouched with her compact mirror in hand. Tatum's eyes lock with mine. I offer him a chilling grin. From across the street I watch as all the color drains from his face.

Like an apparition tucked away, I disappear from sight as a large van drives in front of me. The boys tuck me in front of them as we follow Decker down a nearby alleyway. We scale a ladder taking us to the rooftop of a neighboring shop.

We have the perfect aerial view to watch as Tatum frantically crosses the road to get to where he just saw me. He narrowly avoids getting hit by a car.

"I fucking swear I saw her. She was right here!" Tatum shouts to Ana waiting safely on the other side of the road. We duck down to avoid being noticed.

"Well, I think it's safe to say they're definitely paranoid now. How about we head back to the hotel so we can watch the impending show?" Brielle says, nudging my shoulder.

As gorgeous as I feel in the dress Brielle meticulously crafted for me, I can't wait to be free of it. Without the confines of the corset, I can finally take a full breath. I peruse through the drawers, searching for something comfortable to throw on. Finding one of Jasper's tees, I toss it on, inhaling the traces of citrusy santal.

I'm halfway out the door when I remember our company. Turning back, I snag a pair of Beckett's sweats. My men's eyes darken when they see me in their clothes. They make me feel just as beautiful in their baggy clothes as a stunning gown.

Wafts of garlic and tomato sauce grow more potent as I make my way to the dining room. My steps quicken as I eye the garlic bread. Brielle is already pouring me a small glass of bubbly Moscato, while Beckett sets up his laptops in the connected living room. What use he has for traveling with so many is beyond me, but I suppose it's about to come in handy.

With a plate full of chicken parmesan and fried ziti bites, I take a seat on the ground in between Beckett's legs. My favorite part of being here is escaping the rigid meal plan, eating more of what I crave. Jasper trails behind with two noticeably fuller plates in hand. He hands one plate off to Beckett before joining me on the floor. I smile warmly at the gesture.

The once familiar dining room of my childhood home comes to life across the computer screens. With how Beckett arranged them, everyone has a front row seat to the horror show. Every inch of the walls and ceiling are plastered with stolen images of Ana.

Some are fuzzy, clearly zoomed in snapshots of her from security cameras throughout town. Others are clearer, taken personally from the team who have been tailing her; much more up close and personal. There are easily thousands of images. How long did this take?

Chills snake up my spine at the sight. It's creepy seeing it through the distance of a screen, I can't imagine what it would feel like being immersed in it. The centerpiece laid out on the dining table takes the cake.

Scattered along the deep mahogany are dried rose petals, herbs, and small bones. Hundreds of red and black candles litter the remaining space. Sacred symbols and charms are both propped against the candles and hanging from invisible lines.

In the center of the chaos, there's a small dais holding the voodoo doll replica of Ana. Pins and needles are sticking out of the tiny body at odd angles. Rivulets of crimson drip from the pristinely bleached strands into a small mirror collecting a small pool of the viscous liquid. Using her hair stolen from her hairbrush makes this even more perfect.

One screen tracks Ana, as she makes her way through the house. Like Tatum, she's predictable. Since their dinner was interrupted, she will make herself a meal and eat alone in the dining room. If this were any other day, she'd take her normal seat to the right of William at the head of the table.

Without the personal chefs, she microwaves a frozen meal. I have to hand it to her, she's either delusional, or handling his death and lack of funds in stride. Thanks to Beckett, she won't be seeing a dime for quite a while.

We hold our breath as Ana strolls into the dining room of horrors. Anastasia is too engrossed in her phone to notice the shit show she's walked into. It's only when she lowers her phone to pull out her missing chair that she becomes aware of her surroundings.

The shrill scream is never ending. Once it dies down long enough to suck in a lungful of oxygen, her eyes dart elsewhere and it starts all over again. Noticing the doll, her hand flies protectively to her silky straight locks.

Damn, we should have had someone cut it in her sleep.

She frantically goes to pick up her dropped phone, typing away like a woman possessed. When she tries to run away from the madness, she slips. It's no ordinary fall. No, it's the stereotypical cartoon fall of someone slipping on a banana peel. A handful of images are tossed in the air before fluttering down on her like snow. It's only then that I realize they covered the floor as well.

We laugh uncontrollably at her meltdown. Decker assures us the police have been tipped off and won't be responding to any calls regarding that address. I sip my wine, ignoring the pesky voices saying we went too far. After years of her torment, sabotage, and helping me be sold off to likely be murdered, I'd say this is karma.

CHAPTER 23

JASPER

We bask in tonight's success. Beckett massages Esmarie's shoulders as she sips her wine. She has the most adorable flush on her face. I notice her occasionally rubbing her abdomen. Her diet has been nothing but nutritional clean eating, unlike tonight's indulgence. I worry that the cheesy fried food is upsetting her stomach.

Esmarie stands up to grab the trays of cannoli. If her stomach is already hurting, I don't think sugar will help. A smudge of crimson stands out from the white fur rug we're sitting on. I'm already chasing after my little hellion.

Confusion riddles my brain. She can't be hurt, we would have noticed. Cataloging her body, I note the small stain blooming on the back of her pants. We're too far away for me to quickly ask Brielle for advice. My chest tightens as I panic for a solution. I don't want my little hellion to be embarrassed.

A tiny body knocking me to the side solves my contemplation. Brielle is already barreling her way toward my girl. She takes Esmarie's hand while she whispers in her ear. The adorable flush rapidly deepens. Utter mortification crosses her features as her eyes lock on mine.

Due to being malnourished in the basement, her period never returned after her second week in captivity. For the last six months, she's had an entire team dedicated to improving her health. Doctors predicted it would take at least a year for her period to return.

Not wanting my hellion to be embarrassed any longer, I cross the room in two strides. Cradling her face, I desperately want to fix all her problems.

"What can I do to help? What do you need?" I ask.

Esmarie stares at me like a deer caught in headlights, which only amplifies my panic. Turning to Brielle, I demand, "What supplies does she need? I'll go get anything she needs right now."

With a roll of her eyes, Brielle taps away on her phone. I'm about to explode when my phone vibrates in my back pocket. I stare at screenshots of a neon pink box.

"That's the brand she uses. Match the box and the size. I believe in you," Brielle states, patting my back condescendingly as she tows Esmarie away with her.

Returning to the guys, I whisper to Beckett, "Our girl started her period. Don't make a big deal about it but maybe hide the rug and run her a bath." Returning to my full height, I announce to Decker, "I'm going to get some things for my little hellion. I'll be right back."

Decker stops me with a hand on my chest. He slaps cash in my hand. I begrudgingly accept it, knowing it's not smart to leave a paper trail while we're here. I hold out my other hand expectantly, waiting for a burner phone we use while on missions.

The burner phones don't have any saved contacts. It has a program installed that Beckett and Liam designed. It only relays messages to other devices with the same programming installed. If we were to be taken, no one would be able to get anything off it. They'd need a genius hacker to get past the various firewalls and encryptions.

Burner phone in hand, I quickly forward the screenshot of what I need to find. Since I want to get my girl what she needs as quickly as possible, I try my luck with the little shop in the hotel lobby. I peruse the limited supplies. Luck isn't on my side, as they don't even have the right brand. I'm determined to get my girl exactly what she wants, unwilling to make her settle for what they have.

Pulling out my burner phone, I look up the closest convenience store. The closest one is a five minute walk. If I didn't want to draw unnecessary attention to myself, I would run. The fluorescent lights of the store illuminate the dark street. A familiar face turns the corner. Freezing in my tracks, Jett is the last person I want to see. As Sylvester's second, I know he'll recognize me and send the hellhounds to hunt me down.

I see the moment recognition flickers across his face. At least I came alone, and I'm not running into him with Esmarie. In my frantic attempt to pull out my phone before Jett can inform Sylvester, I almost drop it. My fingers desperately cling on. Clicking on the inconspicuous message icon, I send out "303 Igloo". The screen flashes red, indicating the security protocol is in motion.

Jett growls, jabbing his finger against his screen. None of his messages will be going through anytime soon. By sending the three digits and code word, it sends out an SOS alert. My burner phone is essentially a signal jammer now. It renders all devices within a five-mile radius useless. Only devices with the programing will be able to send and receive messages.

When Beckett first explained this safety protocol to us, I didn't take it too seriously. I thought his precautions were excessive at the time. Now, I see it for the genius it is; especially since it means keeping my little hellion safe.

"Jasper. You know we all thought you were dead. Your little stunt put Sylvester in dangerous waters. He was far too lenient with you solely because your brother was his lover, but that's not enough to save you this time. You royally fucked him over by letting that little cunt escape," Jett hisses.

My eye twitches at the insult to my girl. Weighing my options, I contemplate just killing him. Huffing pulls my attention to a man curled up against the brick wall. Okay, it looks like snapping his neck is out of the picture.

Making sure the street is clear of any other pedestrians; I send a quick jab to his temple like a viper striking its prey. I catch him as he crumples to the ground. My knuckles scrape against the rough brick as I prop his limp body against the wall. The man wordlessly passes me a bottle wrapped in a brown paper bag.

"Thanks," I say as I attempt to wrap Jett's hand around the bottleneck.

Patting down his pockets, I pull out his wallet. I toss the man the cash Jett has on him in exchange for his help setting the scene.

With hurried steps, I make my way into the convenience store. At the back of the store, I hold up my phone screen, flickering my attention between the picture and scanning the boxes in front of me. Seriously, why are there so many damn options? Finding what I need, I double check that every detail on the box matches.

My steps falter, as I pass by some heating pads. My hellion was rubbing her stomach. There are some heat wraps that seem like they could help her cramps without having to be next to an outlet. It's a no-brainer to grab them, and I search out some chocolate and snacks while I'm at it.

My foot taps impatiently as I wait for the clerk to scan my items. Through the glass, a familiar van pulls up. Decker leans casually against the hood, but is scanning every inch of the street.

Without saying a word, I toss the bag into the passenger seat before hooking my arms under Jett's armpits. Decker grabs his ankles. Together, we throw him in the back. I leave him to restrain him as I saunter back to the homeless man that helped me earlier.

"Come on. You did me a solid, let us help you." I nod toward the van. I've always been taught to never leave any witnesses behind, but my gut is telling me to not harm this man.

With guarded expression, he hesitantly climbs in back with an unconscious Jett. Decker arches a brow at me, but remains silent. We drive around, making random turns before returning to the hotel to ensure no one is tailing us.

Flipping around in my seat I jab a finger at Jett. "He trafficked my girlfriend. It took a lot to get her to safety. Any objections about us stopping him from snagging his next victim?"

He shakes his head, giving me a proud smile.

"Good. If you're not too attached here, you can come with us. We can set you up with a job, a new life, whatever you need," I offer, hoping Emmett will understand and come through for me.

Glassy eyed, he offers his thanks. After a little bit of coaxing, he tells us his name is Arnold. From behind the wheel, Decker teases me about being a softie. It's all thanks to my little hellion.

Decker, oblivious to my anxiousness to return to my girl, takes his sweet time returning us to the hotel. Arnold takes in the luxurious hotel with a starstruck expression. Two men dressed in the familiar tactical gear take Decker and my vacated seats, smoothly taking off with our hostage.

I leave Decker to get Arnold settled in a room. It's unlikely that we will stay here another night, but the man can at least take a shower, and have a meal. Sorting clothes seems beyond Decker's capabilities, so Arnold will likely be stuck in some loaners for the time being.

Impatiently, I jab my finger into the elevator button. If I knew how to access the presidential suites from the stairs, I wouldn't bother waiting. Lavender permeates the air. The bath was probably the only thing calming my little hellion.

She comes barreling into view, almost knocking me over from launching herself into my arms. Fuck, I'm glad to see she's in a fresh pair of Beckett and my clothes. Unsure of what they told her, I keep my lips sealed. Fear clouds her eyes, and I don't want to inadvertently make things worse.

It kills me to put her down, but she's been waiting long enough. Handing over the bag, she takes it with a beaming smile. While she takes care of things in the bathroom, I find Beckett already packing.

Beckett greets me with a hug. I'm too stunned to initially react, but eventually pat his back in return.

"Fuck, Jasper. We were worried about you. What the hell happened?"

Despite the circumstances, a smile creeps along my lips. I've never heard Beckett curse so much. A punch to my shoulder has me raising my arms in surrender.

"The lobby didn't have what she needed, so I walked to the nearest convenience store. Ran into Sylvester's second, and he instantly recognized me. The only explanation for him being here is they're trying to track down Esmarie."

"Ohhh, please tell me you have the bastard. I'm going to kill him myself," Brielle seethes from the ottoman.

At the news, Beckett runs his fingers through his curls as he paces the room. Mumbling to himself, he resumes packing. His once meticulously packed bags are thrown together haphazardly. I take time throwing together a few outfits for Arnold, which happen to be mainly Beckett's. Sensing our urgency, Brielle helps us pack up the remaining items.

My hellion returns with what looks to be everything from the bathroom in hand. At least I didn't have to be the one to tell her we're leaving early.

Once everything is packed, we escort Brielle to her suite so she can pack her things. It's apparent which bedroom Brielle claimed. Her room is a disaster. It looks like a bomb went off scattering her clothes like confetti. Embarrassed, she waves us away to pack Decker's things.

Predictably, his room is the complete opposite. The closet and drawers are untouched. Tucked away under the bed are his suitcases. Beckett doesn't seem the least bit surprised his associate has been living out of his bags the entire time. Hell, one suitcase is dedicated to weapons. Within minutes, we make one final sweep before placing his luggage by the door.

The girls have managed to collect the clothes into piles. Brielle quickly shoves the smaller of the two into the closest bag before running off toward the bathroom. I'm sure a tornado ran through there as well.

Beckett and I make quick work folding the remaining clothes and tucking them into bags. We occasionally share a side eye over Esmarie's head, questioning where the hell all these clothes came from and if we can leave any behind.

When it's apparent that we aren't stuffing anymore of her belongings into the bags she has, I search for an alternative. Rummaging through the closet, I find a bag the hotel provides for laundry services. Holding the bag open, Beckett scoops the remaining items in.

Not wanting to linger out in the open where we can be spotted, we wait until we get verification that the jet is ready and the valet has our SUV ready. Half the team is staying behind to continue tormenting Tatum and Anastasia. On the off chance there's eyes on us, we want to keep up appearances, so they don't know where Esmarie is.

We meet Decker and Arnold in the lobby. To my relief, Decker already handled new clothes for Arnold. Like this, he looks like the grandfather I wish I had; warm and welcoming. His skin is slightly weathered with age, but underneath the stocking cap, his hair is only peppered with grey.

Shit. Arnold.

Before I can explain our visitor, Esmarie is trembling behind me. Beckett steps in closer as she fists my shirt. Ignoring the awkward angle, I reach behind me, splaying my hand across her back.

"I forgot to tell you, we're bringing a friend back with us." I leave out the part where we'll have a not so nice friend tied up in the cargo hold.

Decker has the audacity to shake his head at my oversight. Arnold keeps a respectful distance from Esmarie as we pile into the vehicle. Three identical SUVs merge onto the road. Once we hit the interstate, the drivers effortlessly weave in and out of traffic, shuffling our position. If anyone is following us from the hotel, they'd quickly lose track of which vehicle we're in.

The chaos settles as we melt into the leather chairs within the jet. Esmarie is still eyeing Arnold suspiciously. Once we're in the air, I excuse myself to call Emmett and explain the situation. Emmett is understanding and assures me that after Arnold is vetted, he'll find him a suitable job.

During the flight, Arnold tells us his life story. He served in Vietnam. He lost his wife to cancer less than a decade ago.

The medical debt, coupled with lingering injuries had left him without a job or home. Esmarie squeezes his hand when he admits that he gave up, hoping the streets would reunite him with his love sooner or later.

As deranged as it may be, if I were to lose my little hellion, I'd eat a bullet within the hour. It's simply not worth existing without her. How I managed my twenty-seven years without her is beyond me. After a while, Decker escorts Arnold to the suite so he can rest comfortably in the bed. I recline in the lounger with my little hellion snoring softly in my arms.

CHAPTER 24

BECKETT

If Jett were any other man, I might feel sorry for him. As soon as we landed, Decker dragged him to the interrogation room in the basement. Emmett and Decker wasted no time laying into him. They are likely beating him to a bloody pulp, leaving the questioning for tomorrow.

Esmarie sits in my lap as Liam and I comb through Jett's phone. I didn't have to waste any time hacking my way into his phone. The cocky son of a bitch didn't even have a passcode. Liam assigns himself messages, emails. Looking at Esmarie peeking at my screen, he offers to go through his camera roll as well.

I go through his documents and scan his device for any encrypted files or apps that could hide information. Jasper gives us a list of code words to add to our search parameters.

The code words are mundane and wouldn't raise any red flags. Jasper could only remember a few specific ones he'd heard over the years, but it was enough to establish a pattern for my software to detect. With them, we hit the jackpot. All the locations of Sylvester's safe houses were under exotic bird species, and the houses he holds the girls between auctions were flowers.

When we tried setting up Sylvester and Ago at the last auction, both of them managed to escape both the police and our men. The only good thing to come from it was that they were too busy saving their asses, they left all their girls unprotected. We rescued thirty two girls who weren't already sold. Esmarie has been the driving force in helping us rescue as many trafficking victims as we can.

She insists on accessing her trust in order to provide them with housing accommodations, as well as the psychological and medical help they desperately need. Emmett assures her it's being taken care of, omitting the fact that he's been taking care of the expenses himself.

Liam and I provide each of them with new identities. It takes a bit more time, but we have our female recruits meeting with each of them to choose a backstory and a new name for themselves. Esmarie insists that this allows them to reclaim a part of themselves that was stolen or forgotten.

As luck would have it, Sylvester himself reaches out to his second in command.

Sylvie: Meet at blue spix's macaw. Need more supplies.

I leave Esmarie with Jasper as I make my way to the basement. The last thing I want to do is interrupt the Boss's fun, but he needs to know we may have just found out where Sylvester is hiding.

Slipping into the room, I take a moment to survey the carnage. It takes them a while to notice my presence, but when they do, smiles creep up their lips. They know I have news.

"Sylvester is at the blue Spix's Macaw."

Deck and Emmett's brows knit in confusion. The bird species means nothing to them. Jett, on the other hand, starts thrashing around, spitting out curses.

"We have the address from Jett's phone and traced the coordinates from Sylvie's text. It's a match. Should we get a team ready?" I ask.

"I want our best men out there. Sylvester isn't getting away for a second time. Decker, have your team ready to go in twenty. Ask Jasper if he'd like to join; I know it's personal for him."

With a nod, Decker is already halfway out the door. Emmett addresses me next while unsuccessfully trying to clean the blood splatter from his face.

"Do you think Liam is ready to be sent in your stead? I would like one of you to stay with my daughter."

"Yes, sir. He's quick and efficient in what he does. Your team is in excellent hands having him be your eyes and ears."

Emmett nods before returning to Jett. Taking that as my cue to go, I take the stairs two at a time to return to my girl. At the top of the stairs, a single gunshot faintly rings through the air.

I half expect to find Jasper preparing to head out. Instead, I find him braiding Esmarie's hair. Shit, I should learn how to do that. She looks so happy.

"Hey, did Deck come talk to you?"

"Yeah. I decided to stay behind. We need him alive in order to interrogate him about Ago. Can't do that if I murder him on sight," Jasper says nonchalantly with a shrug.

Esmarie attempts to turn her head, picking up on his tone. Jasper gently prevents her head from swiveling an inch. Neither of us question him about it, knowing there is a lot of emotional baggage that would ensue from seeing him. There's no doubt a lot of anger and resentment on his end. While Esmarie may think he's joking about killing Sylvester, I know he would do it without hesitation.

Every night, we practice sign language. It's made it easier for Esmarie to communicate with us while showing how dedicated we are to her. We're all still a bit clumsy, but we can understand each other well enough.

Is the team still having fun tormenting Tatum and Ana? she signs.

"Hell yeah, they are. With their phones cloned, I send them fun little threatening messages like clockwork. Then, Liam deletes them without a trace as soon as they close out of the message after reading it," Jasper says, proud of himself.

Lord only knows the creative threats and taunts the man has come up with. They're no doubt out of pocket and diabolical. The man was forced to be a monster after all.

"They've been sneaking in and writing cryptic messages on their mirrors. With a little liquid soap, it's invisible until they shower and the steam fogs up the mirror," I say, signing along as I speak.

I show her the pictures they've sent us in their updates. Saving the best for last, I show her the videos where the two can be heard screaming. Our men then come out of hiding to show what message they left for them. They're all along the lines of: "I know what you did", "This was your fault", "You killed me", or "I'm coming for you".

Her smile delivers an intoxicating hit of dopamine. My heart could explode with love having her in my arms. Esmarie is a little tease, grinding her hips into my stiffening cock. Lost in a lust filled haze, I almost forgot I have Jett's phone in my pocket. The vibration is as effective as a bucket of ice dousing the flames of desire.

> Sylvie: Ago is getting impatient for his doll. What is taking you so long to secure the merchandise?

I'm lightheaded as the color drains from my face. Peeking at the message, I'm hoping to see a different message on screen. Somehow, they managed to track down Esmarie's hometown. Could we have another leak? I hope they were in Montreal because she was stolen from there, not because they had tracked her down.

Desperation claws at my insides as a lurking monster demands to be set free. I've never been a particularly violent man, but I would do unspeakable things to eliminate any threat to Esmarie. A newfound weight to find Ago Avanzo settles upon my shoulders.

Sylvester is hiding out in Serbia, and it will be a while until our men can apprehend him. Liam will have plenty of time to hack into any electronics found in the safe house. Hopefully, one will have answers about where Ago is. All my patience to end this is lacking.

Japer plucks the phone from my trembling hands. He kisses Esmarie before going to update Emmett like a logical operative. Staring off into the void, my obsession flicks open the button of my jeans. She kneels between my thighs, tugging at my jeans. Obliging her silent request, I lift my hips. My hands halt on the hem of Jasper's shirt that drowns her.

I'm self-conscious that I'm not allowed to undress this goddess. The last thing I want to do is make her uncomfortable. The two of us hadn't gone beyond a few stolen kisses without

Jasper's company. I sit back, letting my hands roam under the loose fabric, giving her all the control.

Icy fingers wrap around my cock before engulfing it in her hot wetness. My eyes roll to the back of my head as I sink deeper into her perfect pussy.

"Look at me, Beckett," she whispers roughly.

My eyes spring open, forgetting the fact that I'm buried in her. While quiet, actual words just left her lips. Pride explodes in my chest, delivering tears to my eyes.

"Fuck me," she pleads.

My hips buck up into her as our lips crash together. We break apart long enough to tear the clothes from our chests. I suck a perfect nipple into my mouth, rolling it gently between my teeth. Her moans are like a siren call, luring my cum from my cock.

Refusing to come before her, I flip her to her back. Traces of crimson streak across my shaft. I dive between her thighs, flicking my tongue around her clit. Nothing could stop me from devouring her pussy, not even her period.

Her hands push my head away in a weak protest as her thighs lock around my head, preventing me from going anywhere. She comes on my tongue with trembling thighs.

Before she catches her breath, I thrust my cock into her once more. I fuck her slowly. My fingers entwine in her hair. I see my devotion in the reflection of her hazel eyes. Her hips roll up to meet me thrust for thrust. Perspiration glistens across our skin as moans escape our lips on every hard exhale.

Letting go of her hips, my thumb finds her clit. God, I've watched her touch herself so many times, I know exactly how to play her body to bring her to the edge. Our bodies feed off each other, demanding release.

"Oh fuck. I love you, Esmarie. Fuck!" I cry out as I come deep inside her.

Either my words or orgasm set off an explosion in her pussy as she coils around my cock like an anaconda. I'm not embarrassed about my admission. I've withheld the words for so long, it's freeing to have let them go. Admittedly, telling her I love her for the first time in the midst of my climax isn't the smartest move. I can only hope she realizes just how true my words are. To eliminate any doubt, I'll just have to show her with my actions.

CHAPTER 25

ESMARIE

Beckett loves me. I'm glad he shifted us to spooning, so he can't see the emotions playing out across my face. His confession is hard to process. I'm wondering if he really meant it, or if it was just in the moment. If it were genuine, can I even say it back?

I haven't told them, but I've been working on freeing my voice in therapy. I can manage a few sentences here and there, but it's strenuous on my vocal cords.

The light in his eyes when I whispered to him was priceless. I just hope he keeps it a secret. I want to surprise Jasper too. Part of me feels empty not having him here with me. When we first arrived at headquarters, he never left my side. Now, he's comfortable leaving me with Beckett.

Jasper returns to our room with a grim face. Our blissful bubble was nice while it lasted, but it had to pop eventually. I hold my breath, wondering if jealousy will take over seeing us in our state of undress. It's one thing to be in a relationship with me, accepting that I'm also dating another while you're there. It's another thing to know I fucked my other boyfriend while he was gone.

There's a sparkle in his eye as he climbs into bed.

"Did you come inside her pussy? Fuck, I want to breed you, my little hellion. I want to pump you so full of cum your womb has no other choice than to accept our offerings."

My cheeks flame as Beckett chuckles beneath me. I'm not sure if kids are something I want, but I see the gleam in their eyes when they make little comments about fucking me till I'm swollen with their offspring. At first, I thought it was just a joke. Considering they keep their cocks buried in me after stuffing me full, they may be serious.

They won't get any objections from me, but I will remain on birth control for the time being. If they manage to impregnate me while on it, then I suppose it was meant to be.

Jasper hitches a leg over his hip, meeting no resistance sliding into me. There's no guiding his cock to my entrance, just a confident thrust of his hips. I swear it's his talent. While he's not as big as Beckett, he fucks me hard with a wild urgency. It drives me absolutely wild, knowing I'm the only one who's had him.

His fingers grip my hip hard enough to leave bruises. He fucks me with intensity blazing in his amber eyes. Jasper rolls us until I'm straddling him. I bounce on his cock, rolling my clit against his pelvis before lifting back off. He growls as he bucks up into me.

Beckett casually pumps his cock as he watches us. God, why is watching them pleasure themselves so hot? A slap to my clit snaps my attention back to Jasper. I let out an undignified yelp, causing him to deliver another slap. My yelp morphs into a moan, as the pleasure overrides the pain.

There's no hiding the eagerness as my eyes plead for more. Jasper's eyes leave mine to flick over to Beck before refocusing on mine. Pressure increases as Beckett presses a finger into my pussy alongside Jasper's cock. Beckett keeps it there, allowing me to ride them both. All too soon, his finger disappears. He nibbles a kiss behind my ear as he presses his digit into my ass.

My hand shoots out, wrapping around his cock. I corkscrew my hand along his thick cock as he pumps his finger into me. Jasper takes over, fucking me from the bottom. I cry out as a powerful orgasm hits me suddenly.

With a firm hand at the back of my head, Jasper crushes his lips on mine as he fills me with his release. I release Beckett as I collapse onto Jasper's chest, panting hard as his cock twitches inside me. All of us moan as Beckett releases a hot stream of cum onto my pussy where Jasper and I are still connected.

Jasper pumps me on his cock a few more times as if to fuck some of Beckett's addition into me. I fantasize what it would be like to fuck both of them at the same time. Would that even be something they would want? I've never done anal, but I've always enjoyed it when they slip a finger in my ass.

***

We're eating dinner as a family, sans Decker. Brielle is tense, knowing he's going after Sylvester. It's easier for me to be a part of the conversation using the computer my psychologist gave me to artificially generate my voice.

"I want to take everything from Anastasia. She doesn't deserve to live in the house as if nothing is wrong. I want that place to burn down alongside all the memories that reside there. She deserves to lose everything like I did."

That estate never felt like a home, and I now know why. What we didn't know was that there was an entire team waiting to give me the life I was always supposed to have.

"I can take care of that, dear, don't you worry," Arnold promises with a wink.

Although I was hesitant about Arnold in the beginning, he's become the group's grandfather. Turns out he knows a lot about bombs and weapons. He and Decker have far too much fun getting new toys to play with.

Police haven't found William's body, and they likely never will. Since there's no body, the police can't determine if he's dead or missing. Not that it's stopped Ana from trying to get a death certificate so she can inherit everything left to her in his will.

"I'll transfer the deed to the estate to your name, backdating it so it doesn't raise any red flags. Actually, I'll set everything to go to you. You don't have to accept anything, but at least it won't be going to Anastasia," Beckett offers.

"Backdate that shit to the day of her wedding. It'll look like a wedding gift or guilty gesture since he didn't have the decency to show," Brielle adds bitterly.

I feel validated knowing all of them see how greedy Ana is. She will no doubt file an insurance claim faster than my men can bring me to orgasm.

Growing up, she could do no wrong in my father's eyes, and his influence spread to our peers. They made me the black sheep of the family, and everyone blindly followed their lead.

Ana has been whining to anyone who will listen that she's struggling, all alone without Daddy's support. If she'd just get a job, she could afford necessities. Instead, she's been leaching off Tatum. Hell, I bet without the estate to crawl back every night, she'll guilt or blackmail Tatum into letting her move in with him. He may just be paranoid enough that he'd rather be in her constant company than be tormented alone.

Beckett's plan is genius. If the estate is in my name, then regardless of if Ana files, the payout will go to me. The property has to be worth at least two and a half million. I could start an organization to help rehabilitate trafficking victims.

"Can you make it look like an accident? I don't want problems with the insurance payout. I want the money to go toward the girls we've saved. Maybe we could use the funds to double our efforts?" I plead with my father.

Arnold looks slightly disappointed, as if he was hoping to blow it to smithereens. My father just sighs heavily, already working out the logistics of recruiting more loyal men to infiltrate the police force and auctions.

"Can I pull the team tormenting Tatum and Anastasia? I'd like to reconvene with everyone when Decker brings Sylvester back. I want Ago Avanzo dealt with as quickly as possible," my father states grimly.

I'm surprised to see him looking at me questioningly. I suppose it's my revenge plan that has a small team away. My cheeks flame, guilty that those men have been away from their families to do my bidding. Worse yet, my father has been fronting the bill to keep them there.

As if sensing my spiraling thoughts, he continues, "Don't feel bad, darling. They're more than enjoying themselves, laughing through our daily updates. If you ask them when they return, I'm sure they'll tell you it was the best mission they've been sent on."

"Okay," I quietly agree.

My shoulders relax at his blinding smile. I want to make more of an effort to talk to my father. Every time I sign or use my laptop to communicate, it looks like the weight of the world weighs him down. My silence is a constant reminder of how much he failed me, sending me to be raised by William.

"Please tell me we're going back for those two! Give them a false sense of peace, then boom; one last confrontation from the ghost of their past," Brielle schemes, tapping her fingers with a feral smile.

CHAPTER 26

JASPER

Beckett and I are in the middle of a scandalous version of combat training with Esmarie. Emmett is adamant that we still resume training. So, logically, we're stripped down to basically nothing. She needs to be prepared to fight in any condition. If she's naked, she can't freeze up in embarrassment. Heels and a formal gown are next on the list later this week.

She doesn't know I've been lurking outside her appointments, where she's been working on using her voice instead of the generated assistance. Her voice is raspy from disuse compared to the melodic tone from when fate first brought us together.

Taking advantage of my distraction, she delivers a punch to my kidney. Oh, if my little hellion wants to play dirty, I'll oblige. I tackle her to the ground, softening the blow at the last second. I pin her to the training mat with my hips. Her pupils blow wide, wiggling her hips as she feels my erection pressing against her center.

I'm trailing kisses down her body when Beckett's phone goes off. It's the ringtone reserved for Decker and Emmett. Sighing, I nip her hip bone before dragging her up with me. Leaning down, I steal a kiss. With her head cocked back with her proximity, she twirls in circles, returning my kiss as I hover over her.

The more she heals, the more her personality blossoms. An unexpected goofy side of her comes out more and more as our presence gives her a sense of safety and security. Beckett smiles warmly at the display, putting his dimples on display.

"Decker and his team secured Sylvester. Their ETA is ten minutes. Let's get cleaned up and meet Emmett. Love, you can stay with Brielle if you'd like?"

My teeth grind, expecting her to disagree with being separated. She nods dutifully before dragging me with her to our pile of clothes. Relieved that she's not going to put up a fight, I allow her to pull me along. If she asked, I would give up taking my pound of flesh from Sylvester. I'll give up any opportunity for revenge if she so much as looks disappointed for me to leave her. I'll double my revenge on Ago, who will inevitably be next.

We walk her to Brielle's room before making our way to the basement. Emmett is waiting for us, lining up trays of tools ranging from knives, hammers, pliers to torches. Anything you could use to inflict pain; he has at the ready.

Metal screeches as I drag my rolling tool tray filled with my favorite torture instruments toward the center of the room. I want to be the first thing Sylvester sees when he enters, given he's conscious. Pressing my palms to the stainless steel, I launch myself up onto the table. Boots pounding down the stairs signify their arrival.

Leaning forward with my arms locked out, I swing my legs like I don't have a care in the world. Decker, the professional he is, has him stumbling through the door. Good, we don't have time to waste waiting for him to regain consciousness.

Sylvester's black eyes meet mine as I smile maniacally at him. He lets out a breath upon seeing me, shoulders drooping slightly. It's a facade. We all know he's not relieved to see me alive and well. If anything, he likely thinks he can manipulate his ties to my brother to get him out of this.

Hatred flows through my veins as he tosses me a crooked smile. Emmett casts me a calculating gaze, wondering if I've been pulling one over on him all this time. That simply won't do; I intend to be his son-in-law.

Hopping off the table, I shove it out of my way before lowering the chains from the ceiling. Neither Decker nor I are gentle as we string him up. He crashes to his knees once we step away. The whirling of the chains rolling back up into the pulley. When his tiptoes are millimeters from lifting off the concrete, I finally stop.

The false comradery drifts away as lets us see the monster he is. His lip curls in disgust.

"I should have killed you the moment I lost your brother. You're a pathetic waste of space who caused more problems than it was worth. A real man wouldn't sell me out. But I suppose you're not since you couldn't even function properly to break in the girls," he snarls.

If we didn't need him to talk, I would carve out his tongue. He acts as if the morals I maintained in that hellhole are something to be disgusted by.

"Tell us where Ago is," I say, not rising to his baiting.

Bones crunch as my fist connects with his jaw. His defiant eyes bore into me, not breaking contact as he spits blood at me. Shrugging, I peruse the table of goodies. He can keep his answers for now. It gives me time to release my inner demons.

A normal person would select pliers to rip out the nail beds. It's Torture 101. Instead, I select a hand torch and a bastard file. These amateurs are confused about my intentions. I cock my head at an unnatural angle as I watch the flames consume the tip of the file. The metal morphs into a spectrum of yellow, red, and purple as the flames heat it.

Satisfied, I march over. Kneeling, I tear off his shoes, locking his foot between my biceps and forearm. Not wanting him to miss out, I re-submerge the metal tip into the flames. Sylvester, having caught on by now, tries to squirm out of my hold. Shill screams escape his lips as the tip slips under his toenail.

The hiss of his searing flesh soothes part of my fragmented soul. I don't relent until I reach the end of the nail. With a flick, the toenails scatter on the concrete. While everyone processes, I reheat the file, removing every other nail in the same manner.

Proud of my work, I look over my shoulder at the others. Beckett looks like he's going to be sick. Emmett looks almost impressed, and Decker is holding back his laughter. Nodding toward Emmett, I take my place beside them.

Beckett excuses himself to put his skills to use helping Liam, but not before shattering Sylvester's kneecap with a hammer. The three of us spend the next hour using him as our personal punching bag as we ask him useless questions. We all know we won't be getting anything out of him.

I'm dripping in sweat in front of a bloody and bruised Sylvester when Beckett returns. We've knocked out all his teeth, as well as removed the remainder of his nails and a few fingers. Given his rattled breathing, I suspect a broken rib punctured his lung.

"Your good friend Ago will be joining you soon," Beckett states with a triumphant smile plastered on his face.

"Nighty night," Decker says right before he delivers a blow to Sylvester's temple that knocks him out cold.

Arnold is waiting for us at the top of the stairs. "The jet is being refueled as we speak. Weapons are loaded and ready to go."

There's nothing Arnold loves more than putting together bags full of weapons for each of us before we head out on a mission. It's a mercenary's version of a goody bag.

"Beck, I need you with us for this one. Ago is not getting away this time. Jasper, will you stay behind and guard the girls?"

"Yes, sir. I can set up one of the guys to monitor the surveillance here, so we have eyes on the girls while we're in the air."

I hide how excited I am to be left behind. Shivers crawl up my spine thinking about what they may be walking into. Although I'll be the third wheel to girl time, my little hellion's presence will settle my demons.

I care more about these guys than I thought possible. I can't let them walk into his cave of horrors without warning them.

"Ago is one sick fuck. It's unlikely to be a rescue mission alongside his capture. Once he's promised a doll, she becomes his fixation. He likely held onto the corpse of his last victim while he waited for Esmarie to be brought to him. Whatever fucked up shit you can imagine, multiply that by a hundred to mentally prepare. Just be careful."

"Fuck. Thanks for the heads up, Jasper. Let's say goodbye to the girls quickly and grab our bags." Emmett sighs.

The first thing Emmett and Decker drilled into us when I arrived was to always have a bag packed and ready to go. It makes sense in times like these when they want to head out on a moment's notice.

We find the girls with goop covering their faces as they watch a rom-com. Emmett is the first to hug his daughter goodbye, quickly followed by Beckett. Emmett nods at me while Beck claps me on the back in a bro hug.

"All of you better come back in one piece," Esmarie manages to croak out with teary eyes.

"We will, baby girl. I promise. You just got us, you're not losing us," Emmett assures her before slipping from the room after one final hug.

Beck looks shattered as Decker all but drags him from the room. All the fight leaves my little hellion, and she collapses in a fit of tears. My arms catch her before she hits the ground. I smooth down her hair as she clings to me.

"They'll be okay. How about you smear some of that blue goo on my face and resume the movie?" I offer. I'd do anything for her to stop crying.

Arnold wisely says nothing when he finds the girls painting my nails black, my hair pushed back with a headband preventing my hair from getting in the face mask when he delivers snacks. He settles in to join us. I'm glad I'm not the only one left behind. Arnold can distract Brielle so I can steal some alone time with Esmarie. I plan on thoroughly distracting her with my cock and tongue until Beck returns.

CHAPTER 27

BECKETT

Not wanting the others to find out about the cameras I placed in our rooms, I stick to hallway and common area cameras. Decker is tense with reluctance to have Emmett with us. While it would have been best if he'd stayed behind, I understand why he insists on joining.

He wants to personally take down the sick fuck who had tried purchasing his daughter. Emmett is torturing himself further, needing to see for himself the horrid conditions that could have been Esmarie's fate.

Knowing the coordinates of where Ago is, I pull up surrounding surveillance and property deeds. The man isn't in hiding, but rather, he's relaxing in his primary residence. We thought with the failed raid and the feds breathing down his back, he would've gone into hiding. In a way it makes sense; Ago thinks he's untouchable.

Satisfied that there is no suspicious activity around his estate, I hack into the government's database. Finding what I hope is a current floor plan of his mansion, I forward it to the burner phones of everyone on the plane.

Moving to my next task, I try to find a way into his server. If I can hack into his system, I can take control of the gate surrounding his property. If Ago catches onto our arrival and tries to flee, he'd have to flee on foot or by air.

In any case, I could easily hack into its navigational system and have the GPS take him to an alternate location.

Within the next hour, I found the backdoor into Ago's system I was looking for. Covering my tracks, I begin rerouting all his security controls. When we land, I can dismantle all alarms, change all passcodes, and loop their security feeds with the click of a button. I, of course, will have full access to the live feed.

I'm about to start spying inside Ago's compound when my phone vibrates. It's a picture from Jasper that has me chuckling. He is posing with Esmarie, both of whom have their faces covered in a blue goo. They have matching pink fluffy headbands pushing back their hair. I can almost hear my girls giggle as Jasper sends another shot capturing him showing off his black painted nails.

Having caught Emmett's attention, I hand my phone over. He shakes his head, laughing softly. I know he was having his doubts about him when Sylvester was brought in, but there's no denying how infatuated Jasper is with Esmarie.

After his brutally creative torture tactics he inflicted on Sylvester, it was apparent he's on our side. Jasper is more than capable of protecting the girls. The man has managed to surpass Decker in combat in the past months.

With a long flight ahead of us, I update Emmett and Decker of my progress before getting some much needed sleep.

***

Gentle shaking has me rousing from my dreams of Esmarie. I do my best trying to hide my erection, praying whoever woke me didn't notice. My cheeks flame as my hand taps around in search of my glasses. The fuzzy blob in front of me comes into focus as the glass slips in front of my eyes.

Given the easy-going expression on Emmett's face, I wasn't moaning out Esmarie's name, giving away what I was dreaming about.

"We have about an hour until we land. Mind running one last surveillance sweep and getting everything ready?"

I nod before rubbing away the tiredness from my eyes. I'm surprised I managed to sleep the remainder of the flight. My little obsession has been keeping me awake at night. I can't help but watch how peaceful she looks asleep, sandwiched between Jasper and I.

Switching into work mode, my fingers fly across my keyboards. The air strip is at least a twenty minute drive. Hopefully, it's far enough away that it won't raise any red flags with Ago's team. Shortly before we arrive, a false alert will be set off within Ago's compound.

Hopefully, most of his guards will be sent to deal with the breach, and I can lock them in one location then we can easily incapacitate with one of Arnold's gas bombs. For Esmarie's sake, I'm trying to avoid a shootout.

The first team of Decker's men ditch their vehicles just shy of the gates of the compound, hiding them in the tree line. I've already looped their security footage so they won't see us coming. I wait in the armored van with the second team.

Once Decker and his men take out the guards and slip past the gate, I send off the alert. Monitoring their progress through body cams, I wait until they're inside before opening the gate for the second team to drive in.

Closing the gate behind us, I filter through Ago's cameras to pinpoint his location. An hour ago, he was seen going into his basement. I send directions to the first team, so they can retrieve our target as efficiently as possible. There was no sign of a panic room or alternate escape route other than the one inside the master suite on the third floor.

Minutes tick by as I wait for the guards to fall into our trap. Once I'm confident all responding guards are in place, I lock them in before they can figure out it was a false alarm. Furthermore, I block their radio signals before sending half of the second team out with gas masks in hand to deal with the trapped guards.

I focus my attention once more on the video feeds in front of me. I'm limited to a laptop and a tablet I can take with me if I need to leave this van. I search for any signs of any guards roaming the property on my laptop, using the tablet to focus on Decker and Emmett's body cams.

The one thing I haven't been able to access are the cameras in the basement. It's unlikely that there are none, especially if that's where he keeps his captives. Given what Jasper shared, it's more likely he has them set up on a separate, more secure server.

Unable to find any traces of a ghost server, it's no wonder Ago has evaded the feds for so long. If I wanted any private servers, I wouldn't be able to do it from the safety of the van. Since it is a large compound with security, it's bound to have a control room to monitor the surveillance. Reviewing the blueprints once more, I try to narrow down where it could be located.

The chill of the air nips at my exposed skin as I make my way into the concrete fortress. With my tablet in hand, I keep an eye on Decker and Emmett. They know they are going into that basement blind, fine with the risk so long as they capture Ago. I hold my breath as I watch them file down the stairs.

I creep through the abandoned halls, peeking into each room I cross. At the end of the hall, a metal door looms ominously. The door is locked with a biometric scanner. It only takes a few minutes for me to bypass it. A soft click sounds as the lock disengages. Tucking my tablet into the side pocket of my cargo pants, I pull my gun from its holster.

While I don't particularly like firearms, Decker has put me through rigorous training. I sigh with relief when the room is clear. Soft whirring comes from the back of the small office. Inspecting the wall closely, faint traces of light peek through the baseboards. My gut clenches as suspicion creeps up my spine.

My weapon is partially raised when a hidden door bursts open. A burly man in a red uniform charges at me. Without hesitation, my finger squeezes the trigger. The man would make even Deck look small, and I take the brunt of his weight as he tackles me to the ground.

Paleness creeps along his face as he struggles to get a firm grip around my throat. Using his disorientation to my advantage, I wiggle my gun between us. He's too focused on suffocating me that he doesn't notice my gun.

The sound of the gunshot is muffled between our bodies. I wince as the recoil punches into my chest. Warmth seeps over me as the full brunt of his weight collapses onto me. His hands fall limply from my throat as I struggle to push his dead weight off me.

I suck in a large gulp of air, wincing as I do so. The scent of blood permeates the air, leaving behind a metallic taste in the back of my throat. I leave bloody boot prints in my wake as I approach the monitors.

Pulling out my tablet, I check on Decker and Emmett. The screen is cracked from the impact of being knocked to the ground. Closing out of the server, I look for any additional server boxes, and come across an external hard drive. Pocketing it, I continue my search. Hidden in the skeletal framework of a printer, I find a wireless server.

Retreating into the office, I search for an adapter cable. The server's login screen flashes on my tablet. I lounge at the desk as I allow my program to hack into the system. With a ping, I'm in. Camera feeds of a dingy basement pull up. I quickly inform the team that I found cameras in the basement.

"No need, it was empty," Decker's deep rumble comes through my earpiece.

My brows furrow. I see the man I recognize from mugshots as Ago wandering around.

"No, that can't be right. I'm watching Ago dig through a deep freezer right now," I argue.

"Maybe there's a hidden door. From what Jasper shared, Sylvester held the girls captive in a basement below what one would presume to be the basement since it was an underground level. What if Ago has the same thing?" Emmett counters.

Uncaring about leaving traces of my being here, I hook the server up to the closest monitor. I'll just take it with me when I'm done. My fingers fly across the keys as I type line after line of ingrained code. Quiet shuffling comes through my earpiece as they make their way back to the basement they just cleared.

Finding the scanner to the hidden door, I direct Decker to its location.

"It's just a painting, Beck. Are you sure?" Decker asks hesitantly.

If I were anyone else, I'd be annoyed at his doubt. Ago went through a lot of trouble hiding what he's doing in the basement. It's no surprise the entrance to his torture chamber would be well hidden.

"Run your hand along the edges. It's a fingerprint scanner, so it'll be small and inconspicuous. Ago just went into a room."

"Found it. What now?" Decker asks.

"Press your thumb to it. I'll override the biometric denial, granting you access."

I smile smugly as Decker mumbles "Holy shit" under his breath. It seems as though there are only two rooms in the lowest level of the compound. Not needing to tell them to proceed with caution, I remain silent.

On the screen, blood covers the walls. Squinting, I can barely make out the words. It's apparent that someone tried to scrub away the evidence, but the words "I won" are a faint taunt. Movement in the corner steals my attention. Ago is pitoning his hips into a tiny body as he stabs into the remains of another girl.

I don't get a chance to warn my team what they are about to walk into, too busy emptying the contents of my stomach onto the floor. I hear the muttered curses as they experience what

I'm watching in person. Sounds of a fight break through my heaving. Pulling myself up, I check on everyone.

Decker has Ago restrained as Emmett slips a needle into his neck, knocking him unconscious. The remainder of the team in the room are either gagging or throwing up. I can see the state of decay through the camera mounted in the corner. I gag once more, unwilling to consider the fuming stench that must be assaulting them.

With the target apprehended, I disconnect from the server, alerting the team. The second team finally passes through the gate, meeting Decker to take our target off their hands. Everyone else will sweep the compound, searching for anything we can hand over to the authorities. Sylvester won't be the only one Ago obtained his dolls through. Ago is a big fish, and is bound to lead us to more trafficking rings.

Sweeping through the office doesn't offer much beyond the external hard drive and server box I've already found. Shuffling through the desk is useless until I knock against a false bottom. I effortlessly pick the lock. Reaching in, my fingers brush against smooth leather.

Pulling out the leather-bound journal, I open it to expose its contents. It's more like a scrapbook of pages of paper he'd ripped out and taped in. Each page reveals different handwriting, each one a diary entry.

This must be his trophy book of his victims. The sick fuck made each of his victims rehash their torture before finally killing them. On the back of each entry is a recipe. Jasper said he had cannibalistic tendencies, but having the proof in front of you is another thing. I won't be eating meatloaf or a roast anytime soon, that's for damn sure.

"Hey Deck. Hate to ask this of you, but you mind peeking to see what's in that freezer?"

Through the camera I first found Ago through, I watch as Decker slowly peels the lid to the deep freezer open. Shaking his head, he slams the lid shut muttering.

"Nu-uh, Nope. Absolutely not. I know we were hoping to give his victims' families closure, but the forensic team can sort that out," Decker grumbles, delivering a solid kick to Ago before dragging him up the stairs.

I reluctantly pocket the journal before making my way toward the others. Unease churns in my gut at the idea of Esmarie reading the journal. What if it just traumatizes her further instead of helping her move forward? Regardless, the torn pages are going to be removed from the recipes. The ride on the plane will give me plenty of time to figure out a plan. I'm ready to return to my girl. I want nothing more than to hold her in my arms and never let her go.

CHAPTER 28

ESMARIE

In the quietness of the night, I tell Jasper that I love him. Given the sheer number of orgasms he's given me since Beckett left, I'm surprised he doesn't pounce on me again. Instead, tears fill his eyes. Jasper just holds me, whispering all the reasons he's in love with me.

I've never felt safer than guarded in Jasper's massive arms. Well maybe with Beckett here too. I miss having both my men surrounding me. I'm locked in between Jasper's arms watching a movie, when our door creaks open. Jasper, being the protector he is, is stiff and on high alert. I, on the other hand, am hopeful it's my missing piece returning.

Familiar dirty blonde curls peek around the corner and I spring from Jasper's lap. Quick as lightning, I cross the room, launching myself into his arms. Beckett catches me easily.

"I missed you, my love. We're all back, safe and sound," he whispers in my ear.

Blinded by my excitement, I left Jasper high and dry. I search him out, guilt weighing heavy in my gut. I expect to find a hurt expression on his rugged face, but he's smiling at the two of us so hard his dimples are peeking through.

Beckett sits us next to Jasper, who places a reassuring hand on my thigh.

"It's good to have you back, man. This one was getting antsy for your return. Our little hellion slept in your clothes and sprayed the pillow with your cologne every night."

Heat licks my cheeks at Jasper's admission. Luckily, Beckett just chuckles while pressing a kiss to my forehead. That won't do, I need his lips on mine. As if sensing what I want, his lips dance with mine.

Engulfed in his familiar notes of iris and sandalwood, the kiss becomes more heated. I'm desperate for him, and I need to be closer to him. Beckett's erection presses into my thigh, causing me to want to rip his clothes off.

I wiggle off his lap, clawing at his belt like a crazed woman. Jasper pulls off Beckett's shirt with a knowing glint in his eyes. I pop to my feet and kiss him deeply in thanks before returning to my mission to free Beckett's cock.

I want to see a happy dance when I return to my knees to find the damn belt undone. Beckett lifts his hips as I yank his jeans down. I focus all my enthusiasm into bobbing my head along his massive length.

"Oh fuck. Fuck. Fuck baby, slow down," Beckett moans.

My eyes lock with his, telling him I will be doing no such thing. I suck his cock like I'm a dying woman, and the only thing that'll save me is his cum.

Beckett holds my hair out of my face. His pupils are blown wide, only leaving a sliver of green exposed. He lifts his hips, fighting the urge to fuck my throat. The extra push causes me to gag around his cock. His eyes roll back on a moan. I love how vocal my men are. Nothing is more of a turn-on than hearing how much pleasure you're giving them.

I hum around him, as Jasper's fingers slip between my thighs. I didn't notice him moving from the couch, let alone stripping down. Beckett curses as he explodes down my throat. I greedily swallow every drop of his offering.

"Sorry, love. Jasper, fuck our girl and give her the orgasm she deserves."

My pussy contracts at his demanding tone. Jasper salutes him before pulling me away from Beckett. He sits propped against the couch before lowering me onto his cock. Effortlessly, he slides home. I waste no time riding him. My attention keeps getting drawn to Beckett's cock, inches away from my eyeline. The wicked smile Jasper gives me, lets me know his sitting here was intentional.

"Use those pretty little words to tell him what you want," Jasper encourages.

Jasper pistons his hips up into me, hitting that sweet spot. Instead of being frustrated at him pushing me, I release a moan. A pinch to my clit has me lost to the pleasure, reminding me of his request.

"Touch yourself. I need you to come again."

Beckett's cock twitches, already at half-mast. He fists his cock, stroking himself languidly. Turning my attention back to the cock I'm grinding on, I entangle my tongue with Jasper's. As my pleasure heightens, I ride him harder.

A whine escapes my lips when Jasper pulls away from our kiss. Before I can protest further, he turns my attention to Beckett. He's holding out his hand that should be wrapped around his erection. Without thinking, I spit on his hand. Smiling, Beckett resumes fucking his hand.

Jasper holds my attention on Beckett, while nibbling kisses along my neck. His breaths come harder against the sensitive flesh. Knowing he's close, I flex around him as I massage Beckett's balls.

"Come for us, Esmarie," Beckett rasps.

That's all it takes for me to shatter deliciously for them. They follow me right off the edge. Beckett's release paints his abs. Unable to help myself, I lean over to get another taste of him. Beckett's abdominals flex under my tongue.

I've been deprived of this man while he was off hunting down the man who has been threatening my safety. I need to figure out how many times I can make Beckett come tonight.

Jasper chuckles before pulling me in for another kiss. Thank fuck he's never cared about tasting himself or Beckett on my lips. If anything, it seems to turn him on even more.

"Beck, our girl is going to need your cock to wake the fuck up."

Still connected, Jasper carries me to his bed, yanking Beckett with us. Dropping us onto the plush mattress, Jasper looks pained as he pulls out of me. Beckett takes his place in between my thighs. He guides his cock through my wetness, whimpering from the overstimulation. He stares, mesmerized as Jasper's release leaks out of me.

With a growl, I'm flipped to my hands and knees. Resting my chest on the silky sheets, I arch my back, putting my aching pussy on display. Beckett once again glides his cock between my thighs, teasing me. Each thrust of his hips causes his head to rub against my clit.

Feeling Beckett's cock harden with each swipe is blissful torture. Empty, I shatter against him. As if that was what he was waiting for, he enters me with one brutal thrust before I can come down from my high.

Rising, I loop my arms behind his neck. His hands cup my breasts, pulling my back closer to his chest. Beckett is trembling behind me, determined to pump me full of his seed. I watch, transfixed, as Jasper positions himself in front of me. With a tight grip, he fucks his fist as his mouth latches onto my sensitive bud.

Beckett releases a string of curses as his cock glides across Jasper's tongue as he fucks me. I'm pulled away from the sight as Beckett crashes his lips on mine.

"I'm going to come, baby. God damn. You feel so good," Beckett whimpers against my swollen lips.

"Not yet," I plead. "I need both of you filling me."

His thrusts slow as he tries desperately to hold off his impending orgasm. In the next second, Jasper's cock is positioned at my entrance. It's not entirely what I meant, but I shouldn't be surprised that Jasper would be inclined to come in my pussy once more.

Beckett pulls out halfway as Jasper presses in alongside him. He catches my screams at being stretched to new heights. A shudder works its way through Jasper as I bite down on his lower lip. I forgot all about his admission of liking pain with pleasure, and I feel like I've been depriving him of what he really wants all this time.

They work together to fuck me. I'm so close to the edge, but I hold back my release just like Beckett. His self-restraint is admirable because I'm delirious.

"God dammit. Jasper please tell me you're fucking close. I can't hold back any—"

I deliver a sharp slap to Jasper's balls, causing Jasper to crumple into me on a whimpering moan. In a chain reaction, Beckett is cut off as Jasper's cock twitches as he erupts inside me instantly throwing me off the edge of oblivion, taking Beckett alongside me.

My vision blackens and I become lightheaded as the intensity of the orgasm refuses to waver. Both my men fight to remain firmly planted in my pussy.

"Fuck, we should do double penetration more often if it'll make her squirt like that for us," Jasper pants.

My body goes limp as I rely on them to hold me upright. Resting my head on Jasper's broad chest, I listen to his pounding heartbeat. I don't have enough energy to attempt to voice my agreement.

The two bicker quietly over who needs to pull out first, both wanting to stay buried in my pussy. Jasper eventually concedes. Beckett lays us both down, holding onto me tightly. Jasper lays in front of me, stroking my hair as if I'm the most precious treasure he's seen.

***

I wake to my men snoring softly next to me. A sense of wholeness fills me. Unable to fall asleep, I make my escape from the tangle of limbs. Part of me wants to wake them up with my lips wrapped around their cocks, but I think better of it. I rang them for orgasm after orgasm last night, and they're likely still sensitive.

On silent steps, I make my way to Beckett's connected room. Not only do I not want to wake them with my shower, but I don't want to tempt them into joining me. Something pokes out of Beckett's bag, looking entirely out of place.

Curiosity draws me closer. Pages flutter to the ground as I tug the zipper the rest of the way open. Ignoring the papers, I suck in a harsh breath seeing the bloody clothes he has bagged. My eyes close, trying to remember if I saw any injuries. There's none that I recall, but I was drunk with desire for him.

The paper crinkles in my fist as I snatch it up as I storm back to Jasper's room. My hesitance is long forgotten as I rip the blanket off their sleeping forms. Light from the bedside lamp stings as it illuminates the darkness.

My perusal of Beckett's body for injury halts on a purple blossom speckled on his chest. I fight the urge to jab my finger in it for him withholding the fact that he was hurt. Panic blurs my vision wondering whose blood that was.

As if sensing my eyes on him, Beckett's eyes flutter open. Connecting on the papers clutched in my grasp, panic floods his features as his eyes go comically wide.

"Why were your clothes bloody?" I demand.

When he stares at me instead of answering, I poke his bruise as tears fill my eyes.

"Shit. The blood wasn't any of ours. I'm okay. We're all okay," he promises. Staring at each other in silence, I try to decipher if he's lying.

"Esmarie... Did—did you read those? Can I have them back? Please, baby? I forgot those were in my bag. They should've gone with Emmett."

Frowning, I go to examine the paper in my hands. Startlingly, Beckett is in front of me in the next instant, blocking the papers from my view.

Our commotion finally roused Jasper from his slumber, and he's glaring daggers at the man desperately pleading with me.

"Beck. I swear to fuck if you don't start explaining right now—"

"I found some journal entries Ago made the girls write. They're fucked up, and we're all going to need therapy for what we saw there. I dunno, I grabbed them thinking— I don't know what I was thinking. I thought they might bring you closure knowing what you escaped, but now I'm worried they'll do more harm than good."

Beckett spirals before our eyes, pulling at his loose curls. Unable to sit still, he begins pacing the room. Too busy freaking out, he makes no move to steal the pages from me.

"Whoa there, Beck. Just breathe, okay, man? Little hellion, do you think you're in the right mental space to read some fucked up shit?" Jasper stares at me, demanding nothing but honesty. When I nod, he continues, "All right, then we will all be here for you while you do so. Beck, come sit down and hold her while she reads them."

"Do you want Brielle or your dad here with you? They're your support system too," Beckett offers.

I shake my head, wanting him to see that the two of them are enough for me. While I love my best friend, I'd rather be vulnerable in private with my men.

"We can share them with the others later. Let's just take one thing at a time," Jasper offers, picking up on my hesitation.

Already knowing what the pages contain, Beckett buries his face in the crook of my neck. His arms are bordering on painful with how tightly he has them locked around me. Jasper hides his emotions behind a blank mask, and I wonder if he has any idea of the horrors we're about to read. He rubs soothing circles on my thigh, offering his silent support.

We sit in silence as I'm thrown into the worst, and possibly, last moments of Ago Avanzo's victims. I don't miss the fact that they're all signed by the "doll". Suddenly, the guards' taunts all those months ago make a lot of sickening sense. My men sit stoically as I allow hot tears to fall, feeling every ounce of pain and heartbreak, these girls were forced to relive as they wrote about their worst moments.

With one look back at Beckett, I know that there's way more than what I have in front of me. These must just be the most recent. Hopefully, we can bring justice and closure to their families.

"Decker and Emmett are taking care of him. He won't be able to hurt anyone ever again. I promise we are going to do everything we can to bring peace to their families and go after every single one of his connections," Beckett swears vehemently.

Dear Diary,

I wish I was dead. Better yet, back in that cage. At least there, I was left alone and got food and water. Like clockwork, he comes in and beats me until I'm unconscious. I think the sight of my blood arouses him. I wake up to him pounding into my limp body. If I cry, he rapes me harder. If I dissociate, he slices into me.

Every time I beg for food, I get the same answer. I can eat if I willingly suck his dick. I'm ashamed to admit I gave into hunger. His cum was like battery acid, and I didn't hesitate to purge it onto the ground. He beat me as he forced me to lick it off the dirty ground. The only thing worse than the taste of his cum is my stomach acid mixed with his cum.

Instead of a meal, he sliced off my fingers and shoved them down my throat. It's what ungrateful whores get. When I choked on them, he hacked them into smaller pieces. He spent the night stabbing holes into my body and shoving his cock into each one. Every night when he finally leaves me, I pray for death.

-Doll

Dear Diary,

The evil man found out he purchased a pregnant doll. He didn't like that. I naïvely thought he was looking out for my baby's health when he brought me food for once. He crushed pills to make me miscarry into my food. Naked and tied up, there was no way to curl in on myself to alleviate the excruciating cramps. I also had no way of crossing my legs in a meager attempt to staunch the bleeding. God the blood. There was so much blood.

The remains of my baby laid at my feet for days before the evil man returned. He scooped it up without a word. I should've known by his smirk that he was up to no good when he returned with a plate. The grilled blob was unidentifiable, but he promised it would help me regain my strength.

It was only when I finished that he revealed that the mysterious meat was my unborn baby. He beat and raped me for hours for allowing someone else to touch what was promised to him- like I had a choice back in that cage. I miss my cage. With the exception of a few guards, I was left alone. I see my suffering was only delayed and compounded.

-Doll

Dear Diary,

I was sold into hell. The man before me is a devil. I'm no stranger to beatings from my pimp, but this is so much worse. I fear he is going to beat me to death. Yet, I know my death won't save me from this torture. He'd finally rape me, or more specifically my corpse.

The remnants of the girl rotting in the corner is a testament to that. I'm not sure what she did to anger him so much, but he brutally fucks every hole of hers and the ones he's made every day. If swiss cheese were a person, it'd be her.

I wonder if she starved to death like I am, or if blood loss took her first. I'm desperate for anything. I wake up to every nerve on my body being on fire. The mouthwatering smell of grilled meat should've been a red flag. His evil smile as he pried my jaw open should've been another. He stuffed my mouth with thin strips of meat until I had no other choice than to chew.

The devil cut larger chunks for himself. A noticeable bulge grew in his pants as he moaned around the forkful. I tried to move away but couldn't. I didn't notice the pool of blood I was laying in. Precisely cut strips of flesh have been removed from my arms and stomach, exposing the bloody tissue below. I think he made me eat myself.

There's no escape for me, even if I wanted to. Maybe if I never noticed the foot by the little grill I wouldn't have looked down and this wouldn't be real. But I did, and now I'm stuck with bloody stumps right under my hip where my legs used to be. He even cauterized them so I wouldn't bleed out. Lucky me.

-Dolly

Dear Diary,

The man who purchased me under the guise of benign my savior is a demented fuck. I understand why I was left alone. The bastard wanted to break me himself. The gleam in his eye makes me want to pluck his eyes out.

Somehow, he knows exactly who I am. He says he can have my baby sister brought here if I don't lose my defiance as he taunts me with food. I've been taught to be strong, and nothing will make me submit to him, allowing him to break me.

He has to be bluffing. My family is always in the spotlight. There's no way he can kidnap my sister without a public uproar at her disappearance. I was different. I was the idiot who trusted the wrong man, thinking he cared about me. I missed all the signs of him isolating me and grooming me. He told me if I loved him, I would sleep with the men paying him to spend time with me.

It didn't take long for the devil to have my baby sister tossed into hell with me. I was given the choice. She could take my place and I'd be set free. It was a no brainer to set my sister free. She's innocent.

I was confused when I was uncuffed and handed a knife. Only one of us was leaving alive. When he began unfastening his belt, I had no other choice. I held her close, telling her I was sorry as I made it as quick and painless as I could. I hope my screams haunt him in hell. He made a mistake giving me a weapon. With a determined war cry I aimed at his crotch. I hot flesh, and I can only hope I hit my target.

Prick was so concerned about losing his manhood, he left me all alone with the knife. He can't stop me from joining my sister. I wish I could see his face when he returns to find his little doll. Using my sister's blood, I leave a message for him all over the walls; I won, burn in hell.

-Lost Doll

EPILOGUE

ESMARIE

Six years later.

The aftermath of taking Ago and Sylvester down was pure chaos. True to his word, Beckett worked tirelessly to find all of their associates and accomplices, no matter how minuscule their involvement. After reading those diary entries, I let the boys have their fun torturing them. What they didn't know is I snuck to the basement and injected them with every poison we had on hand.

Beckett told me how strong I was the following morning. He's never admitted it, but I'm assuming he stalked me through the cameras when he woke and I wasn't in bed. We also don't mention that I wasn't alone in that room as I took my revenge for every innocent they tortured. Jasper stood at my back like a wall of strength, telling me which poisons would be the most agonizing before suggesting acids. It's our little secret.

Using Emmett's connections to law enforcement all over the world and Beckett's leads, they quickly dealt with every known associate. Some men who were in the same predicament as Jasper were more than eager to flip on Sylvester and his inner circle. Once cleared, they worked with my team and, by proxy, the survivors to find and remember all the girls that were lost and sold along the way.

Our teams found and saved thousands of innocents. After they reunited with their families, they received all the resources they needed for physical and psychological recovery. For those who didn't have a safe home to return to, the Legacies of Hope Foundation welcomed them with open arms.

My father helped me create the foundation for trafficking victims while I completed my business law degree online. Surprisingly, Jasper and Arnold decided to get their business degrees alongside me in order to help my foundation run smoothly. Since they couldn't complete all their courses online, my father hired professors to give private lectures at headquarters. He has done everything in his power to make up for lost time, and we are now closer than ever. That's how we wound up at the Potala Palace in Tibet.

Brielle beams at me as I stare at myself in the oversized mirror as we get away from the chaos for a moment. After my disastrous wedding when I was freshly twenty-six, I never expected to be in an ivory gown again. The dress Brielle designed for me for my first wedding was a masterpiece, but it's nothing compared to the dress I'm wearing now.

Brielle hasn't lost her love of incorporating corsets into her designs. Pearl studded tulle bows attach to the diamond encrusted straps at the crest of my shoulders, trailing behind me like a second train. Crystals are hand sewn along the corset to mimic the pattern of lace. The train is more of a skirt that connects at the hips, giving the illusion of fuller curves.

My father had flown in world renowned designers to mentor her. Her bridal boutique, once small, is now well known and has locations worldwide. She stood by me through everything, and I'm so glad to see all her dreams coming true.

This wedding is everything my first wedding should have been. My actual father is here and walked me down the aisle. There is no bitter sister sabotaging my hair, makeup, or dress. This time, I'm marrying the loves of my life.

Beckett and Jasper didn't want me to have to choose which one to legally marry, so my father suggested we all get married in Tibet. Although polyandry is legal here in Tibet, my marriage to Jasper and Beckett won't be recognized by the courts once we return home. Our marriage is real for us, and that is all that truly matters.

My husbands, being the supportive and loving men that they are, decided to take on my last name. Once they explained that I missed out on being a Beaumont for long enough and picking one of their surnames would equate to picking a favorite, it was a no brainer. With Beckett's hacking skills, the paperwork for them to change their names is already approved and awaiting our return.

One of the biggest blessings is the family we've created. Although a few boys were rescued, all but one got reunited with their families. An eight-year-old boy had a new home at Legacies of Hope because he had no family to return to.

Jasper and Decker visited him every week when it was apparent he was struggling to cope. When therapy wasn't enough, they stepped him and used training as an outlet. After a few weeks, he declared he wanted his new name to be Archer. Archer quickly perfected Decker's imposing stance and glare, but he clung to Jasper.

It was Beckett's idea for us to adopt him. Knowing exactly how caring and attentive these men were with my own recovery, I knew they would be amazing fathers to the little man who deserved nothing but love and comfort. The first time I met Archer, he said I must be pretty special if I have two protectors and proclaimed himself to be my mini protector.

Jasper has never hidden the fact that he wanted me pregnant with his child and thought that adopting Archer would pacify him for a bit. That lasted all of three weeks. If anything, it made his fixation on breeding me worse seeing me with Archer. Despite how often Jasper and Beckett practiced getting me pregnant, it never happened; even when I stopped my birth control.

Jasper immersed himself in research, wanting to try fertility treatments. With access to the best doctors and modern medicine, I had beautiful twin girls so each of my husbands could be biological fathers. They are polar opposites, with Beckett's blonde hair and Jasper's onyx hair. They both inherited my freckles and hazel eyes.

Initially, we were concerned that Archer would feel less like our son when we told him about the twins. Instead of being upset, he was excited because he knows he's special because we chose him to be family.

Archer was there alongside his fathers for my entire pregnancy. He read to my baby bump every night and continues to read bedtime stories to the twins. It's adorable how seriously he takes his role as the protective big brother.

When we told him we were naming one of the girls Harper, after my mother, my father had tears in his eyes. Brielle cried like a banshee when we named the other twin Blair, after her.

I feel sorry for any boys who take an interest in Harper or Blair. As if Archer isn't protective enough, boys will have Jasper and Beckett to deal with. Archer has taken after Uncle Decker and gets a kick out of flirting with every girl he comes across. No matter what, we aren't short of love or trouble to keep us on our toes.

ACKNOWLEDGEMENTS

I just wanted to give a huge thanks to all of my friends and family that have encouraged and supported me along the way. Bringing my ideas to life has definitely been a journey, but I loved every second of it.

To my readers, thank you so much for your continuous love and support! Thank you for taking the time to read Esmarie's story! I hope you enjoyed reading it as much as I did writing it! It would mean the world to me if you could leave a review as this helps this story find new readers.

About the Author

H.C. Maire is a new indie author from Nebraska. She is trying to sort through all the chaotic stories in her head to bring to her readers. When she is not at work, she spends her time with friends or cuddling with her pup while devouring a good book.